W9-BSU-859

Praise for J. R. WARD and her

BLACK DAGGER BROTHERHOOD series

"Frighteningly addictive."

—*Publishers Weekly*

"Ward brings on the big feels."

—*Booklist*

"J. R. Ward is the undisputed queen . . . Long live the queen."

—Steve Berry,
New York Times bestselling author

"J. R. Ward is a master!"

—Gena Showalter,
New York Times bestselling author

"Fearless storytelling. A league all of her own."

—Kristen Ashley,
New York Times bestselling author

"J. R. Ward is one of the finest writers out there—in any genre."

—Sarah J. Maas,
#1 *New York Times* bestselling author

"Ward is a master of her craft."

—*New York Journal of Books*

By J. R. Ward

THE BLACK DAGGER BROTHERHOOD SERIES
Dark Lover
Lover Eternal
Lover Awakened
Lover Revealed
Lover Unbound
Lover Enshrined
The Black Dagger Brotherhood: An Insider's Guide
Lover Avenged
Lover Mine
Lover Unleashed
Lover Reborn
Lover at Last
The King
The Shadows
The Beast
The Chosen
The Thief
The Savior
The Sinner

THE BLACK DAGGER LEGACY SERIES
Blood Kiss
Blood Vow
Blood Fury
Blood Truth

THE BLACK DAGGER BROTHERHOOD: PRISON CAMP
The Jackal

THE BLACK DAGGER BROTHERHOOD WORLD
Prisoner of Night
Where Winter Finds You

FIREFIGHTERS SERIES
Consumed

NOVELS OF THE FALLEN ANGELS
Covet
Crave
Envy
Rapture
Possession
Immortal

THE BOURBON KINGS SERIES
The Bourbon Kings
The Angels' Share
Devil's Cut

J.R. WARD

PRISONER OF NIGHT

THE BLACK DAGGER BROTHERHOOD SERIES

POCKET BOOKS

New York   London   Toronto   Sydney   New Delhi

The sale of this book without its cover is unauthorized. If you purchased this book without a cover, you should be aware that it was reported to the publisher as "unsold and destroyed." Neither the author nor the publisher has received payment for the sale of this "stripped book."

Pocket Books
An Imprint of Simon & Schuster, Inc.
1230 Avenue of the Americas
New York, NY 10020

This book is a work of fiction. Any references to historical events, real people, or real places are used fictitiously. Other names, characters, places, and events are products of the author's imagination, and any resemblance to actual events or places or persons, living or dead, is entirely coincidental.

Copyright © 2019 by Love Conquers All, Inc.

All rights reserved, including the right to reproduce this book or portions thereof in any form whatsoever. For information, address Gallery Books Subsidiary Rights Department, 1230 Avenue of the Americas, New York, NY 10020.

First Pocket Books paperback edition June 2020

POCKET and colophon are registered trademarks of Simon & Schuster, Inc.

For information about special discounts for bulk purchases, please contact Simon & Schuster Special Sales at 1-866-506-1949 or business@simonandschuster.com.

The Simon & Schuster Speakers Bureau can bring authors to your live event. For more information or to book an event, contact the Simon & Schuster Speakers Bureau at 1-866-248-3049 or visit our website at www.simonspeakers.com.

Interior design by Erika Genova

Manufactured in the United States of America

10 9 8 7 6 5 4 3 2

ISBN 978-1-9821-4352-7
ISBN 978-1-5011-9517-4 (ebook)

Dedicated to the two of you.
Because sometimes, the monster is actually the good guy.
Wait, am I channeling Tohr and Beth here?

Dear Readers,

One of the great things about the world of the Black Dagger Brotherhood is how big it is (that's what she said). One of the not-so-hot things about the BDB world is how big it is.

Prisoner of Night is an example of a story in the world that just demanded to be told. I remember exactly when it downloaded into my brain. I was minding my own business, going about my day, when wha-BAMM! The image of a (naked) (spectacularly so, I might add) male stepping through a sheet of falling water barged through and claimed center stage. He refused to leave. I kept seeing the same clip over and over again: a waterfall, the male stepping through, him staring right at me.

The story spooled out from there, and when I got a load of its twists and turns, I was all in—and I also knew it was a standalone. I was *so* compelled not only by the hero, Duran, but by the fact that he was the "weapon" given the heroine to use to try to free her brother. (I mean, really, how are you going to holster something like that?) (Wait, please don't answer that. I blush easy.)

The way Ahmare and Duran interrelate was another thing I just couldn't get enough of. They're the kind of couple I had to cheer for (and, on occasion, pray for) and I really wasn't sure how things were going to come out. As I've said, when I sit down to put a book on the page, I feel as though I'm not the creator of the story but rather its first reader. And I figure, as long as I'm all WTF happens now?!?!, hopefully the reader will feel the same.

I love the big BDB books and I have every intention, as long as the good Lord keeps me on my feet and able to write, of keeping going with the series. But it's really nice to clear the deck of some of these other couples in the BDBverse who really want the airtime—which brings me to *The Jackal*. We've included at the back of this book an excerpt of *The Jackal* (coming August 2020). Rhage, as it turns out, has a half-brother ('Urprise!), and you wanna talk about some sh*t going down? I hope you'll take a gander at this rocket-launcher of a story—and let me assure you, there's a hero worth falling in love with, a heroine who kicks a$$, and some bad guys who really get it in the neck.

Literally.

But I digress! I want to thank you so much for your support and your reading time. Writing about these couples and the adventures they go on is the best job in the whole world. I am so grateful to all my readers, and I really hope you love this book as much as I do!

Hugs,
J. R. Ward

PRISONER
OF
NIGHT

PROLOGUE

Twenty-One Years, Three Months, Six Days Ago . . .

WHERE IS IT! GODDAMN you, where's it at!" Duran spit blood out of his mouth and spoke over the ringing in his ears. "I'll never tell you—"

Chalen the Conqueror swung his open palm again, nailing Duran's lacerated face like a bat hitting a fastball. But it didn't hurt as much as the other shit they'd been doing to him in this castle's great room. They'd already pulled out his fingernails, broken all of his toes, and whipped his back until strips of his own flesh flapped against his ribs. At the moment, he didn't have the strength to keep himself on his feet, but no worries there—two guards, with grips locked under his pits, were holding him up off the floor.

As his head flopped back into its lolling hang, he shook it to get the sweat and blood out of his eyes. In the hissing, kicking light of the hearth, the male in front of him was stocky of build and ugly of feature, an oak stump with a bulldog's muzzle and a hungry bear's bad fucking attitude.

"You are going to tell me the location." Chalen took Duran by the throat with one of his meat hands. "And you're going to do it now."

"Sorry, not . . . a big talker—"

The conqueror grabbed onto the lower half of Duran's face, squeezing so hard his jaw split and the inside of his mouth was forced between the hard-and-sharp of his molars. More blood welled, spilled, fell on his bare chest.

"Why are you protecting the very male who put you here?" Chalen's opaque eyes searched Duran's expression as if he were trying to extrapolate a map of Maryland in the features. "All you need to do is tell me where that facility is. Your father has something that belongs to me."

Duran waited for that grip to release. When it did, he spit more blood out. "I'm not . . . protecting him."

"Then what are you doing?"

"Making sure you don't cheat me of what's mine." Duran smiled, aware he must look deranged. "You kill him . . . I don't get to. When it comes to revenge, sons win over business partners."

Chalen crossed his strong-man arms over his barrel chest. He was dressed in weapons, whatever clothes he had on underneath the holsters of guns and knives largely hidden by metal. No daggers, though. He'd never been Black Dagger Brotherhood material and not just because he was a mutt according to his lineage: Even among black market thieves, there was a code of conduct.

Not for Chalen. He had no code. Not in the Old Country, and not during his last century here in the New World.

There was only one male who was worse.

No wonder the two of them had made so much money together in the drug trade.

"I will break you," Chalen said in a low voice. "And I will enjoy it."

Duran laughed in a wheeze. "You have no idea what I've already been through—"

Chalen swung that palm wide again, the crack so heavy Duran lost his vision, everything going checkerboard. And then there was a drop in blood pressure, his brain emptying of oxygen, floaty dis-association riding in, a foggy savior buffering the suffering.

The sound of chains moving and gears shifting brought him back to reality. A section of the sweaty stone wall rose by inches, the great weight ascend-ing like a gate, revealing a corridor . . .

Revealing a male who was naked but for a black hood that covered his head.

"I will make you pray for death," Chalen said. "And when you give me what I need, you will think back to this moment. When you could have saved yourself from so much."

Duran exhaled in a gurgle. His body was on fire, the pain burning through his veins, turning him into a semi-living, kind-of-breathing, sort-of-conscious incubator for agony.

But fuck Chalen.

"Do what you will," he mumbled. "I'm not going to give you a goddamn thing."

"I will make you wish you were never born."

As the hooded male came forward, Duran was

dragged over and slammed face-first down onto a table, his torso bent parallel to the floor. Turning his face to the side, he smelled the spoiled meat and rancid fat embedded in the fibers of the planks.

"Already there, asshole."

Chalen's face appeared at table level, their eyes meeting. "He just gave you to me, you realize. He didn't even take my money. Just delivered you here and dropped you like garbage."

"No one ever accused my father of giving a shit."

"You need to know who you're dealing with—"

"I hope you stay and watch this." As Chalen frowned, Duran smiled through the blood again. "I want to be looking at you when it happens. All of it."

"There will be no mercy."

"I don't want that." Duran felt his pants get cut with a knife. "You're on my list now, too. I'm going to kill my father and you."

Chalen laughed, his fangs showing. The one on the left was not as long, as if part of it had broken off in someone's neck. Leg. Face.

"That is not your destiny."

"I will make it mine." Duran began to memorize every pore, each eyelash, all the flecks in those muddy hazel eyes. "And I shall not fail."

"Such optimism. I hope it persists as I look forward to ridding you of it. Last chance. Tell me where your father is, and I will let you go."

"I'll see you in *Dhunhd* before that happens."

Chalen shook his head and straightened. "Just remember, you could have stopped this . . ."

1

Present Day

THERE ARE STILL SECRETS in America. In spite of population density, the internet, modern law enforcement, and the constant intrusion of cell phone cameras, there remain, across this great nation, whole tracts of hill and dale that are largely uninhabited. Uninvestigated. Unpenetrated by the prying eye.

For both humans and vampires.

Ahmare, blooded daughter of Ahmat, drove through the night, alone on highways that rose and fell over the heaving earth of the Appalachian Mountains. She was far from Caldwell, New York, by now, a good seven hours into her trip and close to her destination. She had stopped only once, at a roadside gas station to refuel. She had timed herself. Eight minutes from insertion of credit card to reclose of gas cap.

A human male who had been doing the same to his motorcycle had looked across at her, his eyes lingering on her body, his sexual hunger obvious under the harsh glow of the fluorescent lights.

When he'd sauntered over to her, all cock and swagger, she had debated castrating him both to get him off her back and as a public service.

But she couldn't afford the delay—and more to the point, she might fantasize about doing something like that, but she wasn't a natural born killer.

She'd just learned that firsthand.

The leering bastard did deserve a corrective event, however, and if she'd been hardwired differently, she was exactly the kind of destiny to deliver it to him. Vampires were a far superior species to those rats without tails, so it would be the work of a moment for her to overpower him, drag him behind the gas station, and take out her hunting knife.

The trouble with humans, however, was that

they were an invasion of non-lethal pests, ants intruding on an otherwise enjoyable picnic. And the last thing she needed was a bunch of—what state was she in now? Maryland?—cops with Southern accents flashing their lights and pulling her over ten miles down the highway for aggravated assault because the attendant in that little glass box with the lotto ads all over it had positive-ID'd her.

Which wouldn't be tough. There weren't a lot of six-foot-tall, black-haired, black-clothed females stopping to pump gas at three in the morning. And the security cameras no doubt had the license plate on her Explorer.

So, yup, instead of taking action, she'd told the human with the bright ideas that he'd have more success fucking off than fucking her. Then she'd gotten back in her SUV and returned to the highway, reflecting that her ability to override her aggression for a greater purpose proved another truism in the long list of differences between *Homo sapiens* and vampires: For the most part, her kind had a higher evolved rationality.

Although perhaps that quality wasn't intrinsic to divergences in the cerebral makeup between the two species, but rather the result of the much longer life spans of vampires. If you lived long enough, you tended to put things in better perspective. Stay focused on your goals. Understand that present sacrifice yielded tenfold future gain.

Which explained why she was going to get her far younger brother out of a warlord's dungeon.

Overhead, lightning tripped and fell across the velvet black sky, and just as hail struck her windshield like marbles poured out of a sack, her exit glowed green and white in the headlights.

Getting off the interstate, she traveled over a series of roads that grew narrower and more degraded. By the time she pulled onto a dirt lane ten minutes later, the summer storm was raging, great gusts of wind and lashing rain bending the fat-topped, kudzu-choked trees and releasing them just before they snapped free of their root systems.

And there it was.

Chalen the Conqueror's century-old stronghold in the New World.

Either that or a Disney antagonist had jumped out of a movie to get away from all the damn singing and set up shop in this sweaty forest to kick puppies and scare children.

The stone fortress had high walls with thin slits to shoot out of and defensible positions all along its roofline parapet. The entrance even had a bridge that could be drawn up from a murky moat and locked into place. All that was missing were the alligators—and there was a good possibility they weren't missing.

Oh, look, they were waiting for her.

As she stopped the Explorer in the gravel parking area, two males stepped forward out of the shadows on the castle side of the lowered bridge. They didn't appear to notice the storm, and the lack of visible weapons on them was nothing she was fooled by.

They were a pair of cold-blooded killers. Everyone who worked for Chalen was.

She removed her gun and her knife and hid them under her seat. Then she slipped on a windbreaker and turned to the duffel bag that had ridden shotgun with her for the trip. A nauseous swell made her swallow her gag reflex back into place, but she grabbed the handles and got out. Locking up, she took her keys with her.

The storm pushed against her like an assailant, and she held her ground as she walked through the puddles and the mud. As lightning flashed, she noted the black vines that grew, tangled and leafless though it was July, up the castle's slick stone flanks like the clawing hands of Chalen's many dead.

Was he haunted by his deeds? she wondered. Did he care about the ruin he'd brought to so many?

Ahmare crossed the planks that were slick and smelled like creosote. Peering over the edge, she couldn't see anything moving in the stagnant water.

She stopped in front of the guards. They were wearing mouthpieces that pulled back their lips, exposing their fangs like daggers holstered in their mouths. She expected to get frisked, but they didn't move toward her.

Frowning, she said, "I'm here to see—"

The castle's great portal opened by lifting up, the creaking and grinding of gears so loud that the metal-on-metal screeches drowned out even the thunder. Neither of the guards spoke to tell her to enter, but then again, they couldn't. All of Chalen's guards and staff had their larynxes removed.

Stepping into the torch-lit interior, she found herself in a great hall, smelling ripe mold and old earth sure as if the place were a crypt. No rug underfoot. No tapestry on the damp stone walls. No warmth in spite of the fire that raged in the room-sized hearth. There was only a rough-hewn table, long, narrow, and stained, with a set of benches and a single throne-like great chair at one end. Up above, a chandelier of oil lanterns swung on its chain ever so slightly, the genesis of the movement unclear.

Inside her skin, inside her soul, every part of her was screaming for her to get out. Run. Never come back.

Forget she even knew how to find the place—

Something was dripping, and she narrowed her eyes at the shadows in the far corner, expecting to see bodies hung up on meat hooks, well into the process of exsanguination. No such thing. Only a leak that had formed thanks to a conspiracy between cracks in the mortar and the driving rain. There was also a closed door that had a pointed arch at the top and ugly hinges that must have been fashioned by the huge, dirty hands of an ogre.

She should have brought her weapons in with her. She hadn't even been searched.

Abruptly, an image from childhood came to mind, like an innocent entering a slaughterhouse: her brother just months old in her arms, staring up at her with wide eyes, his little button mouth pursing and smiling. Back then, their *mahmen* had been alive and well, cooking at the stove, and their father had been at the kitchen table, reading a newspaper with the headline "NIXON IMPEACHED."

Ahmare had been decades out of her transition

and in a human degree program for nursing. There had been fear over her *mahmen* safely delivering the second young, but all of that had resolved with the successful birth, and the family's fortune, though meager in terms of material things, had seemed as vast and enduring as history itself if you measured wealth by love and loyalty.

How had she ended up here? How had her brother—

Chains moving through antique gears brought her head around. A section of the stone wall was rising up, revealing, inch by inch, a draped figure covered head to toe in black.

"He will see you the now," an electronic voice said.

The scent suggested it was a female. There was something wrong, however. A smell that was off . . .

Gangrene. Rotting flesh under that robing.

And she was speaking with the aid of a voice box unit.

"I am ready," Ahmare said.

"This way." The female indicated the corridor behind. "Follow me."

Falling in with the female, Ahmare tracked the movements underneath the robes. There was a limp and a dragging shuffle, as if one foot, or perhaps a whole leg, were a useless dead weight.

What the hell had been done to her brother here? she thought.

The hall they proceeded down had a high ceiling and torches in iron brackets every six or eight feet. Rats ran in a tributary off to one side, staying thin and long as if they didn't want to attract attention, shooting over and under each other depending on the north or south of their course. Overhead, cobwebs wafted in drafts like fabric in its last stages of disintegration.

The hooded figure stopped before another door with a gothic point at its apex. The hand that reached out was bandaged with dirty gauze, and it was a struggle for the female to open the heavy weight.

"Proceed," the synthesizer said.

Ahmare stepped through and stopped where she was as she was closed in. Up ahead, on a raised dais, an oak throne faced away from her, its high back carved with twisted figures being tortured.

"Right on time," a thin voice said. "Punctuality is so important."

The dais began to turn with a grind, the throne coming around slowly, and Ahmare tightened her grip on the duffel's straps. Chalen had come out of the Bloodletter's war camp centuries before, honed by that sadistic fighter into a killing machine who was efficient only when he had to be. Otherwise, it was well-known that he preferred agony over any manner of quick dispatch—

Ahmare's breath caught. And then exhaled in a rush.

"Not what you expected?" the murderer said as the dais bumped to a stop.

Beneath a cockeyed crown that was missing its head stone in the front, the contorted and pock-marked corpse slouched on the hardwood was in the final stages of dying. Vampires were not like humans when it came to the aging process. Rather than a slow descent into an elderly state, the species went through the transition to maturity at around twenty-five, and following that, their bodies stayed in a state of prime physical condition until the very end of their lives. At that point, a rapid degeneration took place, faculties failing in a tumble that led quickly into the grave.

Chalen the Conqueror had a matter of weeks. If not less.

A skeletal hand extended out of his black robe and cranked a hold onto the throne's arm. There was a grunt as he repositioned himself, and as the wrinkled and decaying face grimaced, she imagined what he must have looked like when he'd been in his prime. She had heard the stories of a massive male whose brute strength was surpassed only by his taste for cruelty.

It was hard to get there from where he was now.

"Old age is not for the faint of heart." The smile revealed many missing teeth, only one broken fang on the left remaining. "I will caution you of its approach when it comes for you."

"I have what you asked for."

"Do you. Clever female. Let me see."

Ahmare dropped the duffel and unzipped it, making sure that none of her reactions showed. Reaching in, she unknotted the Glad trash bag and put her hand into the black plastic. Gripping matted, blood-soaked hair, she pulled out a severed head, the scent of fresh, raw meat wafting up.

Chalen's laugh was the kind of thing that was going to stay with her. Low, satisfied . . . and nostalgic. As if he wished he'd been the one to do the killing.

"Clever, clever female," he whispered.

That bony hand released its grip and pointed at the cold hearth. "Place it there. I have a spot for him."

Ahmare walked over to a spear that been inserted into a hole drilled in the stone floor. Lifting the head, she positioned the sharp tip at the base of the skull and shoved down. As she forced the impaling, she had to stare into the face of what she had killed: The eyes were open but sightless, the skin gray, the mouth loose and gruesome. Tendrils of tendons and ligaments, like the skirts of a jellyfish, hung down from where she had crudely severed the spinal column.

It had been a hack job. She had never killed before. Never beheaded before. And the effort required to pop the top off the dandelion, so to speak, had been a sweaty, messy, horrific revelation.

As she turned back around, she wanted to vomit. But the human had been a piece of shit, a drug dealer with no morals who had sold bad shit to children. Who had contaminated her brother with a false promise of financial gain. Who made the colossal mistake of setting up and operationalizing a plan to cheat their supplier.

Why did you make me do this, she thought at her brother.

"Tell me what it was like to kill him," Chalen ordered.

There was a rapacious edge to the command, a

hunger that needed feeding, a pilot light that burned within the wasted shell that would never, ever bring a pot to boil again.

"Give me my brother," she said grimly. "And I'll take you through it step-by-step."

2

"YOUR BROTHER IS FINE."

As Chalen spoke, it was a throwaway, a
bunch of mushy syllables he didn't bother to
enunciate well. Like their deal had been forgotten
or perhaps never a priority in the first place.

Ahmare narrowed her eyes. "Where is Ahlan."

Chalen stared at the mounted head, the wilted
flesh over his eyes an awning of age that must have
narrowed his visual field. "What was it like? What

did it feel like as you put your shoulder into the hilt and the blade went in between the vertebrae—"

"Bring my brother to me now. That was our agreement. I deliver proof that I killed Rollie, you give me my brother."

"Old age is a thief the likes even I cannot best."

She put herself in his line of sight, blocking his view of the kill. "Bring me my brother."

Chalen jerked as if he were surprised to find her with him. Blinking, he brushed that skeletal hand across his wrinkled brow. Then he focused on her. After a moment, his eyes narrowed with calculation, proof positive that the male he had always been was still alive inside the elderly shell.

"There is something else you're going to do first," he said.

"I've already gone far enough for you."

"Have you? Really? That's for me to decide, don't you think."

"Bring me—"

"Your brother, yes, you've made that request. I'm not going to, however. Not right now."

Ahmare took a step forward before she was aware of moving, a tide of aggression carrying her toward—

She stopped as a pair of guards stepped out from the darkened corners.

"That's right," Chalen murmured. "You will want to rethink any offensive maneuvers. I may appear weak, but I am in charge here. That has not, and will not, change."

She pointed to the hearth. "I did that for you. You owe me."

"No, four nights ago, your brother stole two hundred seventy-six thousand, four hundred fifty-seven dollars from me, and as is my right, I claimed his physical form as payment for the debt. You"— he pointed to her—"came to me when you could not find him. You asked how you could get your kin back. I told you to kill him"—that finger moved to the severed head—"and you did. What you failed to understand when you agreed to terms was that that murder settled the debt Rollie had with me. It didn't do anything with regard to your brother, so you and I still have a negotiation to get through—assuming you do not want me to torture him to death. Over a period of nights. And send you pieces of the body up in Caldwell."

"Fuck you," she breathed.

Two more guards emerged from the shadows.

Glaring at them, Ahmare crossed her arms over her chest so she didn't do something stupid.

"Such language from a gentle female." Chalen shifted in his throne like his bones hurt. "And all things considered, you are lucky you have something you can do for me. I find it very easy to dispose of people who are not useful."

"You don't need me. You've got this place full of males prepared to do whatever you want. If you have another bright idea, let them carry it out."

"But perhaps that is the problem." Chalen smiled coldly. "I have been using the wrong sex all this time. I am thinking now that I should have put a female to this specific task, and you already have proven you can get a job done. Also, like most females, you have exceptional taste in decor. I have this lovely piece of art to enjoy courtesy of your efforts."

Ahmare looked around the throne room, or whatever the hell he called it. No visible means of escape, and no weapons on her as per instruction. She was good at hand-to-hand thanks to all her self-defense and martial arts training, but going up against multiple weaponized males of her own species—

"Twenty years ago, something very precious was taken from me." Chalen went back to staring at the head. "My beloved was stolen. In the whole of my life, it is the only time I have been violated in such a manner, and I have searched for her, prayed for her return."

"Which has nothing to do with me."

"Then your brother will die." Chalen pushed his half-empty crown back on his balding head, the remaining rose-cut diamonds winking wanly. "You must understand that you are in control of that outcome. It matters not to me whether he is killed or goes home with you. If you bring me back my beloved, I will give you your flesh and blood. Or I will cook the meat off his bones and serve him for Last Meal. What will be, will be."

She heard the chains first. Then the moaning. Both were very far off—coming from below?

With a series of creaks, a section of the floor opened up at the base of the dais, a six-by-six-foot wooden panel she had not noticed sliding back to reveal a subterranean level some thirty feet down.

It was a fighting arena. An old school stone fighting ring, and in the center of it . . .

"Ahlan!" she cried as she lunged forward.

Lit by flickering torches, her brother was naked

between the grips of a set of guards, his head hanging down, his legs pigeon-toed and lax, steel shackles dragging behind his motionless body. Blood rivered down his back, the whipping he'd been given making shreds of his flesh, and she knew by the bad angle of both his feet that his ankles had been deliberately dislocated.

So he could not run.

She dropped to her knees and leaned into the drop. As she opened her mouth, she wanted to yell at him for being foolish and greedy, for staying in the business she'd told him to get out of, for taking the word of a dealer like Rollie, who he should have known not to trust. But none of that really mattered now.

"Ahlan . . ." She cleared her throat. "I'm here, can you hear me?"

"Life is full of moments of clarity," Chalen said in a weak voice. "And I know you are having one now. You will go and retrieve my beloved for me. When you return, you will find that your brother is released into your custody. Both of you will be free to go, all debts settled."

Tears welled, but she did not let them fall as she looked up at the conqueror. "I can't trust you."

"Of course you can. When I tell you that I will

kill your brother if you deny me, I mean it. And further, I swear to you that I will also take you into my custody, whereupon you will find that although the males who are my private guard lack vocal cords, they are otherwise fully functioning. When they are through with you, if there is anything left to kill, I will feed you to my dogs. I only serve the masculine meat to my guards."

Down below, Ahlan twitched and struggled to lift his head. When that wasn't possible, he turned it where it hung, a single bloodshot eye peering up at Ahmare. His cracked lips moved, and a tear escaped, dripping off the bridge of his broken nose.

I'm sorry, he seemed to mouth.

That image of him as a newborn young in her arms returned to her, and Ahmare saw him as he had once been a lifetime ago, chubby-cheeked, rosy, and warm . . . safe . . . as he looked at her with myopic, loving eyes.

"I'm going to get you out," she heard herself say. "Just hang on a little longer . . . and I'll get you out of here."

"Good," Chalen announced as the panel began to reshut. "Well done."

Ahlan started to struggle, legs flopping in panic. "Help me . . . Ahmare!"

She leaned further down. "I'll be back soon! I promise—I love you—"

The arena was closed off and she shut her eyes briefly. Down below, her brother's screams were muffled, an echo of terror that nonetheless resonated loud as a jet engine in her chaotic head.

The conqueror grunted as he struggled to get his frail body off his throne. The robed female with the electronic voice box materialized beside him, holding out a gold cane. She did not touch him, but let him get to the vertical on his own.

"Come," he said. "You must put some travel behind you before the dawn arrives if you are to succeed. Your brother will receive no more attention from my males, but neither will we render him medical aid. It would be such a shame for you to lose him through the failing of his natural processes while you ponder the inevitable."

Goddamn you, Ahlan, she thought. *I told you that there was no such thing as easy money.*

Yet she could not be angry at him. Not until she saved him and nursed him back to health.

"And as a show of good faith," Chalen said with his jagged-toothed smile, "I will provide you with a weapon to ensure your safety and the success of your endeavors."

3

THE CASTLE'S SUBTERRANEAN LEVEL was a maze
of stone corridors, all damp and lit with
torches, following the Igor decor scheme.
There was no air underground as far as Ahmare
could tell, not that she expected ventilation or comfort in a place that didn't have electricity and was
run by a madman who'd made it literally impossible
for his subordinates to argue with him.

In front of her, Chalen traveled on a pallet that
was held aloft by four guards, one on each corner,

the quartet walking in perfect coordination like a team of carriage horses. From time to time, the conqueror coughed, as if the subtle sway—or perhaps the mold on the walls and the rat poop on the floor—irritated his airways.

Ahmare kept track of every left and each right, and all the straightaways in between, constructing a 3-D map in her mind of the compound.

"So you keep your guns and ammo in an armory," she muttered. "Or is it more like a bunker."

"I have many things I do not allow others to be privy to."

"Lucky me."

"You are most fortunate, it is true."

The procession stopped, and a rock panel slid back to reveal another long hallway. This one was unlit, however, and there was a scent to it that was . . . not the same.

"Proceed," Chalen ordered. "And take a torch."

"You're going to let me pick what I want?" she said dryly. "What if I take more than one gun?"

What if she took an entire arsenal, doubled back, and killed the motherfucker right here and now?

Amazing how completely unsqueamish she was at that thought.

"There is only one. You will take what has been

given to you and you will be off on your endeavors, to return with what is mine so that you may leave with what is yours."

"Yeah, I remember the deal." She faced the conqueror. "But you haven't told me where I'm going. Or how I'll recognize the female."

"It will all be obvious to you. And if it is not, well, that bodes badly for your brother."

"This is bullshit."

Chalen's pockmarked face twisted into a nasty smile. "No, it is the consequence of your and your brother's decisions. He chose to steal from me. You chose to intercede on his behalf. You are chafing under decisions made freely, and that is folly considering you could have stayed out of this. You opened these doors. If you do not like the rooms revealed, that is nothing I, nor any other, can help you with."

She thought of her brother hanging like a dead body between those two guards.

"Where is my torch," she demanded.

Chalen laughed softly. "Lo, how I wish I had met you at an earlier time in my life. You would have been a formidable lover."

Never, she thought as a guard appeared beside her.

She accepted a flame-topped torch and stepped into the corridor.

"A word of advice," Chalen said.

Ahmare glanced over her shoulder. "You can keep it. And go to hell."

He flashed that broken-picket-fence smile again, and she knew she was going to see those ragged teeth in her nightmares. "My place in *Dhunhd* is quite well assured already, but I thank you for the kind regards. No, I would remind you that it is considered polite to return things you borrow. You must bring the weapon I lend you back to me in good working order. If you do not, you will find that we have another debt to settle."

With that, the panel slid back into place on a resounding *thunch* and she was locked in.

The torch's hiss was much louder now, and as she moved it from side to side to assess where she was, its heat warmed her face. More glistening walls. More rats on the floor—

Off in the distance, she heard falling water—like a river?

Walking forward, she was careful where she put her feet. The light from the flame did not carry far, the darkness consuming the illumination as a meal long denied. Shadows thrown from such an uneven, flickering source made it seem as though insects were crawling all over the corridor. Maybe they were.

As her neck prickled, she reached up and brushed at it. The sound of the falling water got louder, a rushing torrent.

The corner came without warning, a wall seeming to jump out at her, and she stopped short so she didn't slam into the stone. Reorienting herself, she pivoted to the right and kept going.

The first of the iron bars came thirty feet farther on. The lengths were set into the ceiling and the floor, locked in with mortar and stone, and instinct made her stay more than an arm's length back from them.

It was a cell. Like you would see in a zoo.

And something was in there.

Stopping, she swung the torch in a wide arc. What she wanted to see were racks of guns. Bins of bullets. Halters to strap weapons onto the body.

That was what she was looking for.

The rushing water was so loud, it drowned out—

Torches mounted on the walls exploded into flame, and she jumped with a shout. Wheeling toward the bars, she waved her own light source around, trying to see into the cell. Slivers of some-thing shockingly white caught her eye down on the floor.

Bones. They were long bones, cleaned of meat and lying in bunches, pick-up sticks scattered after a large animal like a cow had been consumed. Or . . . perhaps it had been a guard who had gotten himself "fired."

And they weren't all she saw. There was a strange, shimmering optical illusion about five feet behind the bars, an iridescent . . .

It was a waterfall. A ten- or fifteen-foot-long waterfall cascaded from a thin slit that zigzagged across the ceiling. Storm runoff, she thought. That had to be the source.

"Who's there?" she demanded.

A shape appeared on the far side of the water, looming. As her heart began to pound, her mouth went dry.

"Show yourself." She took another step back. "I'm not afraid of you."

When her shoulder blades banged into some-thing cold and uneven, she realized she'd hit the op-posite wall and was reminded that she was trapped in here. The good news was that there was no break that she could see in the lineup of bars, and they were so closely set, nothing big enough to chew those bones could squeeze through them.

Just keep going, she told herself as she brushed at the back of her neck again. The guns had to be farther along—

Ahmare screamed so loudly she flushed bats out of the dark corners.

4

SPRINGTIME HAD COME IN the midst of nuclear winter.

Called forth by an unexpected presence, Duran's body breached the water that poured into his cell, parting the falling rush, disrupting the chaotic crystal flow. The summer rain was warm as it hit the top of his head and flowed down his long hair, bathing his shoulders and his torso in a respite from the cold that he knew from experience wouldn't last long.

The chill in the dungeon was like the curse he lived under, pervasive and unrelenting, and he would not have gone near the balmy rush ordinarily. The return to the cold he lived in was harder to bear than any brief relief was worth.

It was better to remain in pain than to have to resettle into it.

But that *scent*.

Dearest Virgin Scribe, the scent. It beckoned him forward, stripping him of the adaptive reasoning that warned him not to get warm.

On the other side of the water, he didn't bother to wipe his face of his dripping wet hair. He didn't need his eyes to worship her. His nose told him all he wanted, needed to know. She was sustenance in the midst of his gnawing starvation. A fire that would not burn him. Air in a place of suffocation.

His instincts told him all of this, instantly and irrevocably.

And then she screamed.

The sound of terror wiped away his trance-like captivation, and as the chill rushed back unto him, a squatter reestablishing domicile in property it did not own, his higher reasoning bootlicked his senses out of the driver's seat.

Now he focused through the ropes of his hair,

his eyes piercing the distance and the bars that separated them.

The torch that she held gave off unsteady light,
the orange flames strobing her strong face and neck
and shoulders. She was tall for a female, and solidly
built, with dark hair that had been pulled back. Her
clothes were black, as if she were a huntress in the
night, and they were of a style he was unfamiliar
with, the windbreaker made of something other
than cotton.

With a slap, she covered her open mouth with
her palm, ending the sound she'd made, cutting it
off like a limb from the whole. Wide, pale eyes
framed by dark lashes and brows bounced around
him, taking in his naked, muscled body—and his
many scars—with a mixture of disgust and horror.

Instantly, Duran was devastated on her behalf.
Chalen had sent her down here to be drained dry, a
fawn tied to a fixed point in a forest so a monster
could survive. So unfair. But there was another reason he mourned.

She was the first of the sacrifices, after however
many years of being down here, that he actually
wanted.

Chalen had lived up to his promise those eons
ago: The conqueror relished the suffering he im-

parted, feeding off the anger and the agony he caused his prisoner. And he knew that Duran hated the feedings, these females and human women, all invariably prostitutes who had misbehaved, sent down here for their own punishment.

A twofer for the bastard, as it were.

Except . . . this one was healthy. Uncontaminated by disease. And fully aware, too, her faculties undimmed by the servicing of a chemical addiction—

In a rush, his body reacted to her presence and her purpose, hardening, preparing for contact . . . for penetration.

He almost did not recognize the symptoms of desire. No matter, though. He might take her blood because he had to, because he needed to be strong enough to escape when the timing was right. But it would never go further than that, and not just because he enjoyed pissing his captor off.

As someone who had had no dominion over his own body for the eternity he'd been down here, he struggled enough with merely taking a vein that he felt was not his due. He could not contemplate any further violation, even if the women and females thought they wanted him, and so far, all of them had.

Duran stepped up to the bars and waited. When

no guards came from behind her to raise the gate, he frowned.

A new kind of torture, he decided. *That's what this has to be.*

God only knew what was going to be done to this female, just out of reach but right in front of him. The guards were, as Chalen insisted on pointing out and proving, fully functional, even if they could not speak a word—

The rage that came over him was a surprise because, like any sexual impulse, it was something he hadn't felt for so very long. After all these years, his temperament had flatlined even as his heart had continued to beat, the unrelenting nature of the physical pain and humiliations such that he was non-reactive for the most part.

Endurance, rooted in his revenge, had been his only emotion.

Not so now.

This female was not like the others, for a number of reasons. And because of that, Duran felt a protective rage overtake him.

The kind that could easily murder.

5

———— ✦ ————

AHMARE TRIED TO TAKE another step back, forgetting that she was already up against the stones of the wall. The heavily bearded male in the cell was what she had thought Chalen was going to be, a massive, battle-scarred animal with long waves of wet, dark hair falling past his heavy pectorals, his arms corded with muscle, his legs long and bulging with power. Through the bars that separated them, his blue eyes glowed with menace and his mouth parted as if it were just a matter of seconds before her blood was on his tongue.

And he was naked.

Dear God, the only thing on him was a blinking collar around his thick throat—

As a scent of dark spices reached her nose, it was a shock to like the way he smelled. Given all that menace, stale sweat and the fresh flesh of his victims seemed more up his alley, yet instead, she found herself breathing deep, her body kindling in a way she couldn't understand.

And did not appreciate.

When his nostrils flared, she knew he was scenting her right back, and the purr he released made her think of the sounds lions made.

"Where are the guards," he said in a low growl.

"I'm here for the guns," Ahmare shot back over the fall of the water. "There are no guards."

She forced strength into her voice and kept her eyes on his, even as her heart pounded and her mind spun. She needed to get moving. There was no going back where she'd come from, and surely somewhere past this barely leashed fighter was the weapon Chalen had told her he would give her.

She needed to get it and find the way back to

her car—also figure out where in the hell she was going.

"Guns?" the male said.

"Weapons. I don't know, I'm assuming it's a gun."

Why was she wasting time talking to him? she asked herself. But she knew the answer to that. She couldn't look away from him. In another circumstance, in a parallel universe where she wasn't in some dungeon and he wasn't in a cage like a zoo animal . . . she would have been captivated by him.

Not just because of his body or even those eyes. It was the raw power that poured out of him.

The male's brows dropped even lower and he came closer to the bars. Water dripped off every part of him, his body gleaming in the open flames of the torches, and she wished she didn't notice his skin shifting over all that muscle. Still, there was something undeniably sensual in the way his body moved . . . a promise that he could take the very male-est part of himself and do very worthwhile things with it—

"I've got to be out of my mind," she muttered.

"They let you come down here by yourself?" He looked up and around, as if he were searching for something in the ceiling or perhaps beyond those bars. "Did you escape?"

"I'm looking for a weapon. Chalen told me there was a weapon down here I could use, and when I find it, I'm out of here."

When he reached forward, she jerked back and banged her shoulder into the stone again—but he was only gripping one of the bars, his fist three times the size of her own as he tested it with a clank.

"So you are not for me?" he said.

"God, no."

The male looked both evil and erotic as he stared out at her with his bearded chin tilted down, the blue of his eyes flashing under those brows. "That is a relief."

A relief? *What the hell was wrong with her exactly—*

Okay, she'd clearly lost her mind. Shaking her head, Ahmare started walking again, staying close to the wall, out of reach.

Just in case.

"What else did he tell you?" The male's speech was accented with the Old Country. "Tell me exactly."

"I don't have time for talk."

She held her torch out, trying to will the appearance of racks of weapons from the darkness.

"Yes, you do." He tracked her like the caged predator he was, following on the other side of those bars. "What else?"

Ahmare stopped again. There was something on the wall, hanging from a hook by a lanyard. Closing the torch in, it appeared to be a handheld device of some kind, palm-sized with a single button on it. A detonator? Was this the weapon?

Fucking Chalen.

She took whatever it was off by its cord and was shocked by its heavy weight—

The rattling was loud and she wheeled around. A center portion of the cell was rising up, the dozen or so bars disappearing into the stone ceiling.

The male stepped free. And was even more enormous now that there was nothing between them.

She put her torch forward. "Don't come any closer. Stay back."

Throwing out her free hand, she grabbed for another torch in its wall bracket, that object swinging on its lanyard and hitting the wall—

The male grunted and grabbed for the blinking collar at his throat as his knees buckled and he went down to the stone floor in a heap. Rolling onto his side, he curled in and struggled to breathe, his head cranking back, a grimace of pain distorting his features.

Ahmare looked at the black box. Then focused on that collar as his clawed fingers dug into it—

From up ahead, there was another loud clank, and more chains traveling through gears. Fresh air, unexpected and sweet in the nose, rolled through the corridor, evidence that a passageway out of the dungeon had been revealed and was not far.

The male went limp, though he continued to pant.

She glanced at the black box on the lanyard. Looked again at the male at her feet. In a low voice, she said, "I am looking for Chalen's beloved. Do you know where she is?"

"Yes," came the grunted reply.

Closing her eyes, she prayed for some other logic to rescue her from the conclusion she was arriving at. "Sonofabitch."

"What else did Chalen tell you," the male rasped.

Ahmare turned toward the prevailing, humid breeze. "He told me I have to go get his beloved or he's going to kill my brother. And apparently you're the one who's going to take me to his female and help me get her back here. So come on, get up. I don't have much time."

She put the lanyard on her wrist and wound its length around her hand until she could palm the device and put her thumb on the trigger.

The male's eyes struggled to focus on her. They were unbelievably pale now, the irises tiny as if even the dull illumination from the torches strained his retinas like brilliant moonlight.

Maybe that collar held more than just an electrical charge, she thought as she watched it blink.

"I don't have a lot of time," she said. "We've got to hurry."

As the male pushed his hands into the hard floor, she almost went over to help him, but she didn't want to get too close, even with that collar of his.

He was enormous as he rose to his full height.

"You go ahead of me." She pointed with the torch. "So I know exactly where you are."

"I'm not going to hurt you."

"It wouldn't matter to me if you thought you could. We both know that I can drop you like a bag of sand."

"What did he tell you?" the male said like an incantation.

"Not here. We don't talk here." She motioned around. "I'll bet you he's watching us somehow and he can probably hear us. I have a vehicle outside. I hope like hell we can find it."

A gust from the storm carried more moist July air down into the dungeon.

"Go," she ordered.

After a moment, the male walked forward, and she maintained a distance between them as the floor began to rise. She told herself she measured every shift of his muscle, swing of his arm, stride of his leg, for signs he was going to wheel around and attack her. But that wasn't the only reason she was watching him.

His body was still wet. Still glistening. Still full of deadly promise—

Not now, she told her damn libido. After three years of not noticing anything of the opposite sex, now was absolutely, positively *not* the time to get back on that train. And he was not the right male, at any rate. And goddamn it, she was *not* that kind of a female—

The male had an ass that went on for days.

Daaaaaaaaaaaaaaaaays.

Your brother is going to die, she told herself, *if you screw this up or get killed because you let your guard down around this male.*

That grim reality was all she needed to refocus,

and twenty yards down, they finished their gradual ascent at a plank bridge that was lowered across the moat.

Lightning flashed, the illumination ricocheting along the wet stone walls like a stray bullet, and the male covered his head, ducking as if he expected to be struck, the muscles all over his back clenching hard. And that was when she noticed that his legs were trembling so badly, she doubted he could walk.

Ahmare came up beside him. "It's okay. You're . . . okay."

The male reared away from her, covering his face with his forearms as if he were going to be struck by something. That was when she noticed the fresh wounds on him. They were down both arms in a series of crisscrosses, as if he'd been lashed protecting himself within the last twelve hours.

When nothing hit him, he slowly lowered his guard. He was breathing hard, his eyes glassy and fixated as he clearly struggled with what was reality and what might be some horrible forthcoming trauma.

"I'm not going to hurt you," Ahmare said roughly.

Strange to speak his own words back to him. Stranger still to realize she meant them.

The male looked at the bridge with obvious wariness, as if he were unsure whether what awaited him on the far side was a worse hell than the one he'd been in. But he started moving, his bare feet careful over the wooden planks. She stuck with him, keeping his pace, the rain lashing at them, getting him wetter and her damp through her windbreaker.

Halfway across the moat, another strike of lightning zigzagged across the sky, and that was when she saw her Explorer over by the main entrance. The bridge she'd first used was tucked up tight, not that she had any present interest in doubling back on Chalen.

"That's my ride."

Abruptly, the male stopped and didn't go any further. "I can't . . ."

He seemed overwhelmed to the point of shutdown, the storm, the qualified freedom, the whatever-else-was-going-on-for-him clearly jamming up his brain.

She looked at the trigger box in her hand. "If you don't keep walking, I'm going to have to use this."

He didn't bother glancing over at what she was talking about, and she hated to threaten him. All she knew was she had to get him into her Explorer, and she sure as hell wasn't strong enough to pull a fireman's carry on him.

She needed to save her brother, and Chalen had given her a weapon.

As well as a map, evidently.

6

DURAN'S PRAYER FOR AN escape had been answered . . . just not in a way he could have predicted. Here he was, out from behind those bars and nearly free of Chalen's hellhole, released from his imprisonment—and yet, as the female reminded him of the power she had over him, he realized what liberty he had was not his own.

He had begged for an escape. Had repeated some version of "Dearest Virgin Scribe, let me get out of here" so many times that only the variations of personal sacrifice he had been willing to offer in exchange for his release were greater in number.

So it made no fucking sense that he was on the verge of liberation . . . and yet stuck on this plank bridge where he stood, staring up at the angry heavens through rain that was like getting pelted with marbles, the chorus line of ragged, jagged, loosey-goosey lightning overhead just looking for a place to land.

It wasn't that he was afraid of the storm.

He had lived through worse than electrocution. Hell, they'd even used a car battery on him once.

No, the problem was his brain's ability to process the size of the sky, the scope of the land, the breadth of time. Actually, that last one was the worst.

Down in that dungeon, he'd had no way of knowing whether it was night or day, and so he had lost track of weeks, months . . . years. How long had it been? For godsakes, the shape of that car she told him was hers was like nothing he had ever seen before—just like her clothes. And his ignorance was terrifying in a way he could not explain.

"What year is it?" he croaked.

The female said something, and he waited for the syllables to sink in and make sense. Meanwhile, she shifted her weight back and forth like she was plotting the precise course of her footfalls across the puddled courtyard.

"Please," she said, "don't make me use this."

He looked at what she held up to him. It was the trigger to his restraint collar, the one the guards used on him when they had to enter the cell.

Unlike those voice-box-less males, she clearly did not want to shock him, and he had to give her credit for that. She would do it if he made her, however. Something about her brother . . . and the beloved—

All at once, focus returned to him.

Nothing like revenge as an existential palate cleanser.

Yes, he thought. He would take her to the beloved. What happened after that, however, was going to be up to him, not Chalen.

Duran's body moved before he ordered it to, his arms and legs breaking out into a run, his bare feet slapping across the planks before splashing through puddles and pounding over slick rocks. The car he did not recognize as a car came up to him, not the other way around, some distortion of reality shredding the dimensions of the courtyard and drawing the hunk of gas-driven metal right into his face.

There was a *chunking* sound and the interior lights came on.

"Get in the back." The female opened the rear door for him. "Get in."

Duran dove into the interior, his wet skin sliding on leather until his head jammed into the opposite door, a jarring halt to his momentum. Tucking his legs up, the female shut him in and jumped behind the wheel.

They were off in a blink, and he braced a foot and a hand to keep himself from becoming a fish in the bottom of a boat.

Herky-jerky, back and forth, and then a roar as she gunned them down some kind of coast-is-clear. The vibration of the engine and the bumps in whatever road she put them on traveled through the padded seat and into his body, magnifying aches he knew he had and some that were surprises.

And then came the nausea.

He hadn't expected that. He'd never been one to get carsick.

Closing his eyes, he sat up and breathed through his mouth as if maybe the air moving up and down the highway of his throat was the kind of traffic that vomit couldn't break into.

Bad idea with the lids down. He opened things and looked through the shoulders of the front seats to the female driving.

She had one arm outstretched, her hand not so much locked on the steering wheel's curve as welded to it. Idiotically, he had a thought that he hoped her other hand was on the trigger to his collar. He wanted her to protect herself against all threats, including the one presented by an unknown naked male in her back seat who might just eat her.

After all, only he knew that he wasn't going to hurt her—

Hadn't she said the same thing to him? He couldn't remember. Everything seemed like the blurred landscape rushing by the vehicle, indistinct and out of his control.

In the glow from the interior lights—which included a screen-like TV in the center of the console showing a badly imaged extacto-map of their location—her concentration was so fierce it bordered on violence, her jaw set with aggression, her eyes sharp as blades.

Like she expected a *lesser* to roll up onto the hood and shatter the windshield.

From time to time, she jerked her head around, but not toward him. She looked the opposite way, at the side-view mirror mounted on the outside of her door.

He wanted to ask her if anybody was coming

after them, but he held off. For one, Chalen wouldn't be so obvious if he'd sent them on the mission for his beloved. For another, enunciation of any words was going to be too close to a feather on the back of his touchy throat for him to keep the contents of his stomach where they needed to stay.

Assuming he didn't want to mess up her back seat—

"Pull over," he choked out.

"What?" She twisted around. "Why?"

"Pull over—"

"I'm not stopping—"

"Put the window down then!"

There was a heartbeat, and then a rush of thumping air that reminded him of getting splashed in the face with water from a well-thrown bucket. Lunging toward the opening, he squeezed his shoulders out just in time.

As he gripped the door's edge, his gut spasmed, a great fist vising up and ushering out everything that was inside of him.

She let off on the gas as if she were being kind, but he was too busy to care.

Everything hurt, and that got worse as the sickness continued. It was as if his senses, lit up and excited by all the stimulation newly available to them, couldn't discriminate between the pains in his body and the environment he was in. Everything was too loud, too much, too intense: Wind tunneled into his ears. Rain pelted him on one side. His throat burned like fire.

His eyes watered.

Duran told himself that last one was because of the speed at which they were going.

Some things just didn't bear closer inspection.

When he finally retracted himself back into her vehicle, he was a shaky, cold-sweat aftermath, and he drew his legs up tight to his chest, wrapping his arms around his knees and lowering his head onto the tripod they created with his spine. He'd always been a big male, and there wasn't enough space for all his height and weight in this position, and that was the point.

The tight squeeze made him feel like he was being held.

And not by someone who enjoyed his pain or created it as part of their fucking employment—

"Here."

At first, he didn't notice he was being addressed. But then a water bottle tapped him on the shin.

"Thank you," he said hoarsely.

Cracking the top, he brought the opening to his lips, prepared to wash the taste out of his—

Cool, clean . . . clear.

It was the first uncontaminated water he had had since he had been hit on the head in his quarters at his father's facility and woken up in Chalen's castle of horrors.

Laying his head back against the seat, he closed his eyes and tried not to weep.

7

AHMARE KEPT CHECKING THE back. At first, it was to see if they were being followed. But then it was equally about the prisoner.

After he threw up outside of the SUV, she closed the window a little to cut the thunderous roar of air current. When she looked again, he was sitting all compacted, like a banquet table folded up for storage, his head back, the long column of his throat working as if he were about to vomit again. Hoping to help, she took a bottle of Poland Spring and gave it to him—

The scent of tears was such a shock, her foot let off on the gas once more. She couldn't afford to stop, though. Every instinct she had was screaming, *Run! Run! GTFO!*

"Are you okay?" she said.

The question was a stupid one, but the words were what little ease she could offer him, a way to reach out without touch, a connection that didn't require her to get too close.

The distance wasn't just because he was a dangerous stranger: She didn't have to be a genius to know Chalen was more likely to screw her and kill her brother than be a stand-up gangster and keep his side of their new bargain. Still, she had to work with what they'd agreed to, and he wanted this "weapon" of his back.

The last thing she needed was to bond with another source of chaos, pain . . . mortality. And yet this "caged animal" she'd been so terrified by wasn't looking very "animal" anymore. He was coming across as incredibly mortal . . . and fundamentally broken. Fragile, in spite of his incredible physical strength.

The fall-apart happening in her back seat was a shock. She'd assumed she'd have to be one eye on the road and one eye on the prisoner, playing a game of Bad Idea Blackjack between whoever Chalen sent on their tail and the predator in her car.

Not where she'd ended up. And probably the only surprise so far that didn't work against her.

"I need to ask," she said more loudly. "Where are we going? You're going to have to tell me."

The prisoner put an arm over his face and made like he was wiping sweat off his brow even though they both knew that wasn't what he was doing. He was getting rid of the tears. Then he leveled his head. As his grim stare met hers in the rearview, she looked to the road and hoped she had some sign to focus on. Maybe a deer to swerve around.

Those bloodshot, watery eyes of his were like a black hole sucking her in.

"Where are we?" he asked.

"Damned if I know," she muttered as she looked at the nav screen.

That wasn't exactly true, but apparently her brain decided to answer that one on an existential level.

"The highway's not far," she told him. "You've got a choice of north or south."

With a groan, he unpacked his proverbial suitcase, unfolding arms and legs and sitting forward to focus on the screen. Her body moved itself away, pressing into her door, and even though she tried to hide the shift, he must have noted it because he backed off a little, giving her room.

God, he was so damn big. Then again, she had been working around humans at various gyms for the last two years and even the larger males of that species weren't anywhere near his size. Was he of aristocratic blood? The Scribe Virgin's breeding plan, the one that had created the Black Dagger Brotherhood and the *glymera*, had mandated matings between the strongest males and the smartest females—and even though that had been eons and eons ago, remnants of it still walked the earth.

And threw up down the quarter panels of Ford Explorers.

"We want west," he announced. "So stay on this road."

"How far do we go?"

"I'll tell you. Do you need gas? I can't tell by all that stuff on your dashboard."

She glanced at the tank reading. "We have just about three-quarters."

"That'll be enough." He sat all the way back. "Is there anyone behind us?"

"Not that I can tell. But who knows."

"He'll send guards. He's been trying to find this

destination for—" The prisoner frowned. "What year is it? I know you told me, but I can't remember what you said."

When she gave him the answer again, he looked away, to the darkened window beside him.

"How long did he have you down there?" she asked.

She would have preferred not to go there. She wanted to use him for what she needed, get that female, and go back to Caldwell with Ahlan safe. Details were bad. Connection was bad. Seeing him as anything other than a tool was bad.

He was not her business or her problem. God only knew why he was down there, anyway—

"Twenty-one years," he said quietly.

Ahmare closed her eyes and mourned for the stranger in her back seat.

※

They were on a different rural route now, one that the prisoner had told her to get onto about thirty minutes prior. The fifty-six miles an hour Ahmare was able to crank out made her feel like they were making some progress, and still no one was following them.

At least not in a vehicle. She wouldn't be sur-

prised if members of Chalen's guard were demateri-
alizing at regular intervals, tracking them through
the dense, vine-consumed forest that choked the
road's ribbon of asphalt.

She glanced at the clock. Dawn was coming
soon; they only had another hour at most. And that
was going to be a complication for any bloodhound
guards on their tail, and also for her and the prisoner. The fact that they were going away from the
sunrise cut them a little slack, but not much.

"How did Chalen get your brother?" the prisoner asked.

It was the first time he had spoken since he'd
given her the direction to get on this road.

"Ahlan owes him money."

"If you bring the conqueror's beloved back, it's
priceless to him. Your brother better be into him for
millions."

"I don't get it." She focused on a passing sign.
The town it announced meant nothing to her. "If
Chalen's a conqueror and his female's this close,
why doesn't he go and get her himself or send his
guards?"

"Because torturing me for the precise location
for two decades didn't get him anywhere."

Ahmare felt the urge to apologize, but reminded

herself that his suffering wasn't anything she'd caused—so there was no basis for the I'm-sorry. Still, twenty *years*? She felt like she'd lost two full calendars of her life since the raids and the deaths of her parents. Multiplying that times ten was a time span she couldn't fathom.

"That must have been . . ."

As her words died off, she had a thought language was like a photograph of reality, something two-dimensional trying to capture that which had mass and movement: It was destined to come up short, especially when more than the basic who, what, and where, the surface details, really mattered.

"We're getting close to the turnoff."

"Okay. And then how far?"

"I'll let you know."

Ahmare twisted around. "We're in this together, you realize."

"Only as long as you need me, and if you know where you're going, I become dispensable. Forgive me, but survival is my very best skill thanks to Chalen."

She had never considered that mistrust might be a two-way street between them. With his superior size, she'd viewed herself as the only possible victim if they clashed. Looking at it from his point of view? She was in control of his collar, wasn't she. And Chalen was running the show for the both of them.

"Plus I have someone to protect," the male said.

"Who is that?"

"A friend. Or at least she used to be. We'll see if that's changed."

They fell silent after that, and the country road just kept going, rising and falling over slight hills, the heavy-topped trees forming an arch of leaves above the pavement. As she looked at the clock again, she noted that the canopy overhead was thick enough to block out the night sky, but not even close to being a tunnel capable of shielding them from the sun.

"We need shelter soon," she said. "We don't have much time—"

"Up here, take that right."

Ahmare frowned through the front windshield. "What right—"

She almost missed the gap in the tree line and slammed on the brakes. Her seat belt caught her, and the male put out a hand to stop his weight from getting thrown forward.

The dirt lane was tight as a soda straw, more like a pathway through the kudzu than a real road, and as she penetrated the dense leafy tangle, vines scratched at the sides of the Explorer and everything went green in the headlights. After some distance, a clearing of sorts presented itself.

"Stop here," the male said.

She hit the brakes. There was no structure that she could see, only a semi-absence of anything that had a trunk thicker than her pinkie or taller than her shoulders. Bugs and moths, attracted to the headlights, seizured and sideswiped among the undergrowth, gathering as if by siren call to dance with the grace of computer programmers.

Ahmare put the Explorer in park, but did not turn off the engine. The isolation of the site made her think of horror movies.

"We get out at the same time," the male said. "Do not make any sudden movements. Put your hands over your head and any guns or knives need to stay in the car."

"I'm not leaving my weapons."

"Yes, you are. If you get out with one in your hand, she'll kill you before I can explain. As it stands, she may shoot us anyway."

Ahmare turned around to him. "Where are we and who the hell are we meeting? You're going to tell me or I'm turning this SUV around and—"

"How long do you think your brother's got? Realistically." When she cursed, the prisoner shifted to her side of the SUV and put his hand on the door release. "So, on three, we get out at the same time and pray to the Virgin Scribe that she'll let me speak before she pulls her trigger. One . . . two . . ."

"I'm taking this." She held up the collar's device. "You could be double-crossing me, and—"

"Three."

He opened things up and slid out, holding his hands up and leaving the door wide as if he were using it as a shield.

Ahmare cursed again. She was getting really goddamn tired of being out of control.

Reaching for her own door, she popped the seal and extended her leg. The night air was so humid, it was like breathing water, and the stench of rotting vegetation made the suffocation worse.

This is where they find the bodies of missing human women, she thought as she shifted her weight out and rose to her full height.

Putting her hands up, she sifted through the sounds of tree frogs for approaching footsteps or—

The laser sight's red beam hit her high thoracic area, on the flat plane of her upper chest . . . an impact target that would drop her like a corpse.

Glancing over her shoulder, the male had an identical glowing red dot above his sternum.

"Surprise, surprise," a dry female voice said from within the trees. "Duran back from the dead. Assuming that is you under all that hair."

"I was never dead." The male kept his arms right where they were. "And all I need is what I left here."

The red spot circled on his torso like the potential shooter was considering other sites to bury a bullet in. "You dump your shit on me and then disappear for two decades. When you do come back, it's buck-ass naked with another female. And you expect me to give you anything but a grave?"

"Come on, Nexi—"

"Want to introduce your friend before I put a lead slug in her chest?"

The prisoner looked over. "What's your name?"

Okay, fine, so they hadn't been properly introduced. Like that had been on her radar.

"Ahmare."

He looked back in the direction of the voice. "This is Ahmare. I'm taking her to go after Chalen's beloved."

There was a pause, like that news flash was a surprise. Then the laser sights lowered. "How romantic."

A tall figure walked into the clearing, but stayed just outside the direct beams of the headlights. In the glow, as mist from the storms gathered around her, it was obvious the female knew what to do in a fight. She was built not unlike Ahmare herself, with a body honed by practice—but in her case, you had the sense she'd seen actual conflict because of how calm she was.

Her skin was dark, her hair was black and in a hundred braids, her guns were matched.

Her green eyes flashed like they were backlit, peridots in moonlight.

Holy shit, she was a Shadow.

"So where are your clothes?" the female demanded of the prisoner.

"I lost them a long time ago."

The female's eyes traced his body, clearly noting the scars. "You've added some skin art," she muttered.

"Not by choice."

There was a long silence. "What the fuck happened to you, Duran."

8

N EXI HADN'T CHANGED.

It was a relief and a complication, Duran thought. She clearly remained a killer, a straight talker, the kind of female you didn't bullshit. But she also still did things her way or no way.

"I just need my stuff," he said. "And then we'll be out of here."

"I'm not giving you shit until you tell me where you've been."

This was not jealousy talking. At least . . . he didn't think it was. Their relationship had never seemed to him to be the sort that grew that kind of tangled green vine. Maybe he was wrong, though. Her anger seemed misplaced unless she cared more than he'd thought.

"Answer my fucking question," she demanded.

"Working out." He shrugged. "Night school. I started a lucrative business selling recycled plumbing equipment—"

"He's been in Chalen's dungeon," the female—Ahmare—said. "He was released only so he can take me to the conqueror's beloved."

Duran glared at the interruption. "Shut up—"

"Dungeon?" Nexi said in a low voice.

"For twenty years," Ahmare added.

"Christ."

"More like hell," Duran muttered as he looked way.

Nexi wasn't one for emotion except for anger. She rarely showed anything else, being more interested in exploiting the feelings of others for her own purposes. Then again, after what the two of them had been through, she had learned the hard way that giving people insight into your heart and soul was like loading a gun and handing it over to an enemy.

No reason to believe the intel wouldn't be used against you.

It was, he realized now, why he'd agreed to help her all those years ago. He'd figured someone like Nexi wouldn't get attached to him and that meant he was off the hook for being responsible for anybody but himself. He could go his own way after they were out of where they'd been, the split clean so he could take his revenge on his father.

There had only ever been one thing for him, and that was not settling down with a female.

Still, a part of him didn't want to see that Nexi didn't care—or, worse, was happy—about what had been done to him. He was also ashamed, even though she wasn't aware of any details of his captivity. Back when he'd known the Shadow, when they had worked on their escape, he'd been solid about who he was and what his purpose had to be. Now? This mission that was taking him back to where they'd been held, so long the only goal he'd ever had, abruptly felt like there were two strangers in on the action.

The female he'd just met.

And himself.

"I didn't throw any of it out," Nexi said. "Your shit, that is. It's all where you left it."

"Thank you."

"I was just lazy. It wasn't to honor your memory or anything."

"I didn't think it was."

Nexi muttered something that didn't carry. And then she addressed Ahmare. "You need to hide that SUV. My garage is through there." She pointed to two tire tracks barely noticeable in the kudzu. "I'll open it for you. You're going to leave me the keys in case I want to use it—or decide to chop it up when both of you don't come back."

Nexi dematerialized, up-and-gone'ing it, and Duran looked at his female—

The female, he corrected in his head. He looked at *the* female. At Ahmare.

"We're going to need to camp out overday. There's no way we can get where we need to go before dawn because I can't dematerialize." He tapped his collar. "This is steel."

"Goddamn it." The female glanced at the sky like she was measuring the distance the sun was going to have to spin overhead in millimeters. "That's twelve hours."

"There's nothing we can do about it."

"The hell there isn't. You can tell me where to go and I can do this myself."

"You won't make it out of there alive."

She stepped right up to him. "You don't know who you're dealing with."

"You don't have the access codes or the layout to the compound. The *Dhavos* will know the second you set foot on his property and he'll have you headfirst in a grave before you can get one shot off."

"*Dhavos*?" She frowned. "Wait . . . this is a cult?"

"Set up sixty years ago." Duran shut that door himself. "Back when humans were tuning in and dropping out, the *Dhavos* took inspiration and created a Utopia underground. Like most megalomaniacs, he cared less about enlightenment and more about being worshipped by a captive audience, but he managed to convince about two hundred wayward codependents to join him on a bullshit spiritual journey that culminated in servitude—and not of the holy variety. He's a rapist and a murderer and he pays for everything by selling heroin and cocaine to humans who live below the poverty line."

"I thought *dhavids* were illegal under the Old Laws. The Scribe Virgin never allowed them."

"You think anyone cares about that out here? Why do you think he put the colony in all these goddamn bushes."

"So we're close."

"Not close enough to make a go during the night we have left. Come on, before Nexi changes her mind."

Except the female didn't move. Ahmare just glared around the clearing as if she had X-ray vision and was convinced a good, sharp stare would reveal the colony's entrance.

Duran slapped a sting on his ass and felt a young's satisfaction as he flicked the dead bug off his butt cheek. But when he did the same on his left pec and then his right shoulder, there was no more feeling superior over killing something smaller than him.

"I'm getting eaten alive. Do what you want with this vehicle, but Nexi isn't going to like it if you don't put it where the sun don't shine—and she tends to blow up things she doesn't like."

Something he might keep in mind.

Ahmare's pale eyes locked on him. "I'm bringing all my weapons with me."

"Okay, but keep them holstered. Nexi is not going to appreciate any aggression and she'll deal with it in a way that require stitches."

"You know a lot about her."

"Not really." He clapped his palm on the side of

his throat. "Come on, we've still got some distance to go and I don't like the look of the horizon."

A subtle glow was kindling in the east, the kind of thing that a human might think of as the harbinger of a new day, the pretty precursor to a peach-and-pink departure party not just for night but for the storm clouds that were retracting from the sky as well.

He wished the damn things would stay put for another hour or two. They needed time, instead of some false show of optical-only optimism that would burn them both to a crisp.

Ah, the romance.

9

T HE CABIN WAS OLD and small. The covert security measures were new and plentiful.

Ahmare would have been impressed under different circumstances.

Each of the four windows had iron bars and steel mesh—although only on the inside so as not to attract attention. The front door had no doubt been wooden when the place had been built, but that flimsy option had been swapped out for a reinforced steel vault panel. Motion detectors and security cameras had been mounted in each of the corners, and more mesh covered the walls, ceiling, and floor, ensuring that no vampire could dematerialize into the interior.

She was willing to bet there was an escape hatch somewhere, a way to get underground, but damned if she could find it.

"I'm going to use your shower," the prisoner told Nexi.

He—Duran—didn't wait for a yes or no—or for directions, not that there was any question where the running water was located. He just walked into the closet-sized loo and shut the door.

A low rushing hum came on immediately and suggested he wasn't wasting time, and she appreciated that. But him being efficient with the soap and water wasn't going to affect the velocity of the daylight hours. They were still going to take forever, like a bone healing on a human.

Weeks . . . months. Before mobility could once more be had. Or at least it was going to feel like that.

Ahmare looked across at the Shadow. That the female was watching her, all hunter-tracking-prey, was not a news flash, but come on. And one of the two guns with those laser sights was still palmed.

"You mind putting your weapon back in that holster," Ahmare said.

"You're not in a position to make demands."

"If I was going to come at you, I would have already."

"Tough talk." The Shadow didn't seem to blink, those black eyes so steady, it was as if they were made of glass, like the lens of a camera. "You like old Schwarzenegger movies? Bet that's the closest you've ever gotten to a real fight."

Ahmare made a show of checking out the interior again. The fact that the Shadow had figured out she was a teacher, not an actual fighter, seemed like a portent of failure. Sure, she had been trained in self-defense after the raids, and she had been teaching those skills to others at gyms up in Caldwell. But that was not the same as being a soldier.

Don't think like that, she told herself. *What was the saying? 'Whether you believe you can or believe you can't, you're right'?*

The furniture was all also-ran afterthought. Mattress on a wooden stand. Travel trunk with the lid down. Table and two chairs that were hand-made, but not by someone who cared about how things looked. Then again, this bolt-hole was about war: A workstation housed gun-cleaning supplies and stones to sharpen daggers and knives. Holsters for various weapons hung on pegs. Bomb detonators and sniper rifle tripods lined various shelves.

"You ever kill somebody before," the Shadow asked. "I'm just curious."

"Yes," Ahmare said roughly.

"Oh, fancy. You didn't like it, though, did you? What didn't work for you? The mess? You seem like someone who doesn't like messes."

This is just a conversation, Ahmare told herself. *Given what I'm going to face, this is nothing. No problem. Just words.*

"Or is it the guilt." The Shadow leaned back against the mesh-covered wall of the cabin, crossing one combat boot over the other. "Yeah, I'm guessing you don't like the weight of the dead around your neck. The memories hang like a heavy chain right on your sternum and make it harder to breathe. When you close your eyes, the smell of the fresh meat and gunpowder comes back to you and chokes you. It's all about being robbed of air at the end of the day, isn't it. No more air, no more life. Both for you . . . and him. It was a him, wasn't it. You couldn't kill a young or another female, I don't think. You don't have it in you."

Ahmare's eyes went to the closed door of the bathroom.

Hurry, she thought.

"So who was it? Who'd you send to the Fade."

The Shadow started to flip her gun up and down, casually tossing it and catching the weight as if she controlled every single molecule in the weapon, in herself . . . in the whole world. She seemed, as the Beretta caught air and returned to her palm again and again, to be in charge also of gravity . . . of time itself.

That confidence was captivating in the way of a cobra. Hypnotic because it was—

The Shadow pointed the gun directly at Ahmare's chest. "Answer my fucking question."

—deadly.

Those black eyes flashed peridot, and Ahmare knew with absolute certainty that she was going to fail at getting Chalen's beloved back to him. The Shadow was right. She was a classroom chump, a videogamer who excelled in an armchair but was going to be picked off first in the actual field of conflict.

All target practice, no tried-and-true.

She thought of her brother and mourned him like he was already dead.

The Shadow smiled, flashing long white fangs. "Poor little girl lost in the wood. You think Duran's your hero? You think he's going to rescue you? Let me tell you that he won't. That male is going to desert you when it counts and you're going to end up dead in a place where your kin won't find the body. If you're smart, you'll back that SUV out of my garage and get gone. For someone like you, it's better to admit defeat up front than be forced into a failure that puts you in the Fade. At least if you cry uncle now, you'll still be able to enjoy pumpkin spice lattes and the last season of *The Big Bang Theory* in September—while you're working out at the gym and shooting targets on the range—"

"You're wrong," Ahmare blurted.

"About what?" The Shadow started flipping the gun again, like she had to do something to stave off boredom. "Do tell, on the outside chance I can learn something new about you. But you should know that I catch liars like fish in a stocked pond. And I like to eat them."

"It wasn't a gun. There was no gunpowder."

Those eyes flicked over. Before the Shadow could interrupt, Ahmare found herself speaking in a direct voice.

"And I don't know what I'll see or smell when I

close my eyes because I killed him just after night-fall tonight."

She thought of Chalen wanting to know what it had felt like. When she had denied him the story, failed to fulfill his greed, it had been an act of defiance in a situation she had no leverage over.

Now, she spoke through a tight throat to prove herself.

And not to the Shadow.

"I spent the night before watching the human," she said. "He lived with two other males, but he worked alone, outside of town in a trailer in the woods. I tracked him to his lab. He made meth, I guess. What else could he be doing with all those filthy tubs and chemicals?"

"What did you use," the Shadow said. "If not a gun, then what."

Ahmare reached to her hip. "This knife. Chalen wanted proof he was dead."

"What did you cut off?"

"His head." Ahmare licked her lips with a dry tongue in hopes of getting the syllables unstuck from the sides and roof of her mouth. "I was waiting for him out at the trailer. I spent most of the day practicing in my mind how it would all happen, but nothing went like I thought it would. He had cleared the field around the trailer to get a clean shot at anyone who came on the property—so I had to lay flat on top of the roof, on the far side of the slight tilt. It was hot. The asphalt shingles were like a griddle from being in the sun all day and my palms were sweaty. Maybe that was the fear, too, although I'm not sure what I was more worried about. That he would show up or that he wouldn't."

Everything was so crystal clear, the memories like the glare of chrome, making her eyes and her head hurt even though this was all just a tape played backward, a book's passage being read instead of written.

"I dematerialized behind him after he got out of his car. I don't know how I did it. My plan had been to slit his throat before he knew I was there, but he sensed me immediately and wheeled around. His eyes were wide and glassy—he was clearly high and that's the only reason I got the job done. He was sloppy with his defenses. I was sloppy with the attack. I stabbed at air instead of his chest because he jerked to the left, and then I sliced his shoulder. He went for his gun. I caught him in the forearm . . ."

She closed her eyes. Reopened them immediately. "I dropped the knife. It just popped out of my hand because of the sweat. As it turned out, that was how I took him down. My hands functioned better when there was nothing in them. I punched him in the side of the head. Then I broke his nose. There was blood everywhere. I kicked him in the groin. As soon as he fell facedown on the ground, I got on his back and I didn't let him up. My body . . . it knew what to do."

Ahmare looked at the Shadow. "I watched me submit him. I know that sounds weird, but I swear, I was standing five feet away from myself when I got his throat in the crook of my elbow and started strangling him." She moved her arm into that position, pulling up her sleeve, clasping her wrist, and making like she was pulling back. Then she released the hold on herself and looked at where she had just gripped. "I have bruises right here."

She turned her arm around so the Shadow could see the purple and blue marks. "When I was driving down here, my wrist ached and I couldn't figure out why. But I have my own handprint in my flesh."

Dimly, she was aware that the Shadow wasn't tossing the gun anymore.

"I think he was still alive when I rolled off of him." Ahmare put her arm behind her back, hiding her wrist like that could erase what she'd done. "I mean, he was breathing or at least seemed to be, but he was limp and both of his pupils were fixed and dilated when I turned him over. I sat back in the dusty dirt and caught my breath. Something told me I had to decide what I was going to do then, which was nuts. I had already decided what I had to do. I had spent all day thinking about the steps I needed to take. Yet I hesitated."

She curled her nose. "He smelled bad. His blood was flowing down the lower part of his face and all over his T-shirt, and it was like rotten eggs, all sulfur and rot from the drugs. I told myself he wasn't going to survive long anyway. I told myself that he sold shit to kids that, even though they were only humans, didn't need that kind of thing anywhere near them. I told myself . . . that he was the reason my brother was in Chalen's custody. That what the two of them stole from the conqueror was this male's fault, not Ahlan's.

"None of that seemed to matter when it came down to it. I still don't think I had a right to take his life. A person's heartbeat is their own property. Even thieves and murderers get that gift from the Creator. And I knew . . ." She touched her sternum. "I knew, deep in here, that if I killed him, I was no better than he was. I was the drug dealer to children. I was a corrupter, too."

"So what made you follow through on it?" the Shadow prompted.

Ahmare shivered and put her arms around herself even though the air inside the cabin was warm and a little stale.

"That's the scariest part," she said.

"How so."

She met the other female in the eye. "I don't know what made me do it, and that is terrifying because it makes me think there's something ugly inside of me that I can't control. I tell myself, so I don't get scared I'm a monster, that maybe destiny was using my body as a tool, that the human was somehow getting his due. Or that maybe it was only because I had practiced things so many times in my head, and as long as I never think like that again, I'll never do something like that again. All I know for sure is that I watched my hand reach out and pick up my knife from the dirt. I didn't even wipe the hilt or the blade off. I left all the grit that clung to my sweat on the rubber and the blood on the metal where it was. It helped my grip, I guess, and what did it matter whether the steel was clean or not?" Her lids went down again, but she couldn't bear the images she saw. "I only needed one hand for the front of the throat, but getting through the spinal cord required two and all my strength. Stupid me, I was trying to cut bone instead of finding the juncture between two vertebra. I fixed that by angling the blade differently. And then I felt the knife go into the soft earth on the far side."

The shower went off behind the door, and Ahmare started to rush through the story. This was too private to talk about in front of anyone else—and what a strange thing to think given she didn't know this Shadow any better than she knew the prisoner.

"I forgot a bag." She stared at the scuffed floorboards of the cabin. "All my preparation . . . and I forgot to bring something to put the head in. That's how I found out what was inside the trailer. I'd left my Explorer about ten miles away, in the parking lot of a strip mall full of outlets. If I dematerialized there with a dripping . . . well, the shops were closed, but humans are everywhere, even after dark. So I went inside the trailer. The place was filthy and toxic, but there was a box of Glad trash bags by the sink. I took two, put one inside the other, and went back out to the body. For some stupid reason, I felt guilty I'd only left him one more bag in that box, but really? That was what I was going to apologize to him for? And like he'd ever cleaned up that trailer of trash?"

Flapping from inside the bathroom. Like the prisoner was giving some terry cloth a workout.

"I threw up when I came back and saw him. His blood was running out of the arteries I'd cut, making this dark semi-circle in the dirt, a new kind of head to replace the one I'd taken from him. The fan pattern reminded me of when my *mahmen* had homeschooled me and I'd learned about the Mississippi River and the way it dumps out into the Gulf of Mexico in this shell-like formation of silt under the seawater. I teared up at that point. Somehow that perfectly unimportant photograph from a geography textbook in my childhood was now permanently stained, sure as if the man I'd just murdered had reached his soon-to-be cold hand back through time and gotten his blood on the page. That contamination feels, right now at least, like it's going to spread to every single memory of my happy family and the way things used to be before the raids. I feel like in killing him, I killed everything that was protected by the hard guard of That Which Was Before. Before the *lessers* murdered my *mahmen* and sire, I wasn't like this. I was myself. I was no one who would ever kill anything, and my brother would never have dealt drugs to survive, and Chalen the Conqueror and that prisoner in your bathroom and you and this cabin are all a foreign land with a foreign language I will never, ever visit."

Ahmare rubbed her face. "But it makes sense that I should lose something when I took his life. No matter what my reasoning or justifications, it was not mine to claim, and balance needs to be maintained. He's dead now, and I've lost the previous version of me that I had kept so dear, the last vestige of my family."

Dropping her hands, she looked at the Shadow. "So you're right. I'm not cut out for this. I'd rather teach self-defense, and I do like pumpkin spice lattes. But here's another truth. We don't get to choose all our destinations, and however much I hate that I'm going to have to live with what I did to that drug dealer—and God only knows what else is going to happen—what I cannot and will not abide is doing nothing to save my brother. He's all I have left, especially now that I've lost myself, and however imperfect he is, I'll take him alive over the cosmic nothing I'll have on this earth if Chalen kills him."

There was a long pause as their eyes met.

Then the Shadow holstered that gun and turned away to the refrigerator. "You hungry? I got food we can pack up for you both."

10

DURAN HADN'T BEEN ABLE to tolerate the warm water.

Turning the cheap faucet handle to the inscribed "H" had been a rusty habit. Stepping under the warmth and humidity had been unbearable. He'd lasted for a split second, his body tingling with unanticipated pleasure, before he'd cranked things to "C."

The bad news about that decision revealed itself when he got out: Without any steam, the medicine cabinet's cracked mirror had been as naked as he.

So he caught his reflection for the first time in over twenty years.

Unrecognizable. And that seemed apt.

His hair had been short and his face had been shaved when he'd been captured. Now, the apex of him was a garden overgrown, ropes of black cables falling from the crown of his head down around his shoulders, a beard extending from his jaw and chin well past his collarbones to his sternum. The only thing he saw that he recalled was the color of his eyes. Blue. Pale blue.

A dull, pale blue. Beach glass.

He had some passing thought that he needed to keep everything the way it was now. It felt camouflagey, this self-generated bush he could tuck himself behind. Faulty reasoning, that. Where he and that female were going, he was going to stand out like a sore thumb. A neon sign. A cackle in silence.

As his hand reached up to touch the beard, he watched it pull a stroke or two, feeling nothing of whatever texture was against his palm—hard and crinkly like it looked? Or fool-ya-again soft, in spite of the crimp?

He wasn't sure who had told his arm to rise up.

He'd certainly had no conscious thought of making the move.

Something to keep an eye on.

It was a relief to turn away. Towel off. Reach for the latch to open the flimsy door so he could step out. Some faulty part of his brain decided that his introspection was a function of the small lavatory, and provided he never entered that space again, he didn't have to worry about getting trapped in that cognitive loop once more—which he needed to avoid because he knew where it would lead.

Memories of what had been done to him.

And then the resonance of his current reality: He was either dying or going back to Chalen.

But there wasn't any contest between those two choices. He was going for the former, hard as a sprinter with a canine behind him.

Reemerging into the cabin's interior, he realized he should have set some ground rules for Nexi being alone with the female. Considering what lay ahead, nothing good was going to come from scrambling Ahmare's brain, and shit knew Nexi liked to rewire people—

The two females were standing shoulder to shoulder at the short counter in the galley, passing a package of salami back and forth. Then trading a dull knife to spread mustard and mayonnaise. Next came the plastic-baggie handoff.

They weren't talking. Or looking at each other. But considering the alternative? Better than he'd expected.

"You know where you kept your clothes," Nexi muttered over her shoulder.

"Thanks."

He didn't know what the hell he was thanking her for. It was more like an apology, except why he was I'm-sorry'ing the fact that he'd gotten hit on the head and had woken up on Chalen's play table made no sense.

Because you were going to leave her anyway, he thought as he opened the lid of the trunk by the bed. *And it seems like not only did she know that, but your lack of emotion may have hurt her.*

Duran was quick with getting dressed, pulling on combat pants that had more pockets than slack surface area, as well as a long-sleeved shirt made of lightweight material, and combat boots with almost as much deep-dish tread as they had leather upper. Three of his holsters were in there. He left one behind. Seven of the guns he'd stolen were in there. He left three behind. His ammo belt was still missing two bullets in the lineup, the vacancies together in the middle like a pair of front teeth knocked out.

He couldn't remember why he'd taken the pair out of order. What he'd shot at.

He couldn't remember a lot of things. Which was what happened when you were keeping your eye on a prize.

Lots of things unrelated to your Kewpie doll got missed.

Hello, Nexi.

Duran bent down to close the trunk lid, and as he straightened, he wobbled thanks to a wave of dizziness.

"I wish there was time to feed," he said to no one in particular. Being at his best strength would be a help.

Nexi laughed over at the counter. "I'm out."

I didn't ask, he thought, but kept that to himself. The fuel-to-fire ratio was already high just by his mere presence.

"ATV where I left it?" he said.

Nexi turned away from the food and went over to her worktable. Tossing a set of keys at him, she said, "Yes, and I just drove it yesterday. It's gassed up."

"Thank you."

"You can quit that."

The female, Ahmare, zipped up a backpack. "You're sure we can borrow this?"

"It's his anyway." Nexi went to the door and opened it. "I'm keeping your SUV if you don't come back. Think of it as rent for me taking care of his shit."

"She's not responsible for my actions," he heard himself say.

"She is now."

"It's okay," Ahmare said as she put a key fob on the counter. "That's more than fair. And thank you for the food."

Nexi ignored them both, staring pointedly out at what was left of the night. In the heartbeat of silence that followed, Duran felt like he needed to say something before he took off. The impulse was the same, he supposed, as when you dropped a glass on someone's floor and were compelled to go for the paper towels.

"Don't even think about it," Nexi said tightly. "You want to do right by me, get the fuck out of here and take her with you."

Odd the parallels in life, he decided as he walked out. When he'd left her the last time, he'd known he was going to see her again and had dreaded it. Now, he knew he wasn't going to . . . and he dreaded that, too.

So much unsaid. So many amends that would never be made.

Why did people always learn things about themselves too late, he thought.

11

———◆———

THE ATV COVERED THE increasingly rugged, but no less green, topography with the gait of a bucking bronco and the demureness of Sid Vicious.

As Ahmare held on to a pair of grips by the seat—because the other option was Duran's body— she was bounced around, ass popping up and landing just off-center so many times she developed a core competency in median relocation. Worse, the scream of the engine was doing her nut in. The high-pitched, eardrum-rattling whine was too close in pitch to the anxiety that was vibrating through her body and her brain, the adrenaline load way over her limit.

She couldn't handle one more second of delay. And yet here she was, close to dawn, with nothing but hours and hours of inactivity ahead of her while her brother was in Chalen's custody. It was like a nightmare where you were trying to get home but obstacle after obstacle tripped you up: cars that broke down, blocked roads, missteps of direction followed by locked doors with keys that didn't work.

When her brother hadn't come back at dawn three nights ago, and then hadn't answered his cell phone, posted anything on social media, or showed up by the following midnight, Ahmare had gone into his room in the apartment they shared and pulled open the bottom drawer of his dresser. There, in among his second-favorite concert T-shirts, semi-worn-out jeans, and that flannel button-down that was his go-to starting in September, was a Mead brand business envelope sealed and labeled in his messy handwriting.

"In Case of Emergency."

About nine months before, just as he'd been leaving for the night, he'd told her he wanted to make sure she always knew where he was. She'd asked him what he thought cell phones were for, but Ahlan had gotten serious, for once, and told her about the envelope and where it was. She hadn't thought anything further about it.

That was how she'd gotten in touch with Chalen. She'd called the ten-digit, out-of-state number, and after some routing, found herself talking to Ahlan's "employer."

She'd known her brother was dealing drugs. At first, when tightly rolled bundles of cash had started turning up in his pockets, and a new TV the size of an Olympic swimming pool had been delivered, she'd refused to look too closely at what he might be doing for a living. It had been one of those things, like his sex life with various women and females, that she resolutely refused to think about.

But then he'd started using.

The glassy eyes. The staccato speech. The growing paranoia.

And finally, a human male, Rollie, had begun stopping by.

She'd had to confront Ahlan about the man one night. As soon as that twitchy, toothless, stinky human had left, she'd had it out with her brother and he'd promised he was going to stop. Everything.

Five nights later, he disappeared.

Six nights later, she had opened the envelope. Made the call. Struck the deal.

Tracking Rollie, she had learned about the underage dealing, something that had made her sick because there was no way her brother hadn't done that as well. Then the trailer and the beheading. The long trip to Chalen.

From the second she'd ended that initial call to the conqueror, she had measured time like a Rolex, aware that her brother was a trauma patient and she was the only one-man ambulance who could save him.

Hours counted. Seconds . . . counted.

Except now, after the double cross and Chalen's new assignment of what was probably a suicide mission, she was back where she'd been as she'd tracked Rollie and tried to figure out how to kill him: Waiting with a bomb in her lap, the ticking minutes driving her crazy.

As she was whipped by branches and vines, taken deeper into the forest by a stranger, she tried to figure a way around losing time during the day.

She tapped Duran's shoulder. When he didn't respond, she tapped harder.

His bearded face turned to the side. Over the din, he said, "Almost there—"

"Stop!" she yelled. "Stop now!"

". . . you hurt?"

She'd clearly missed the "Are" at the beginning of that. "We need to think about this! There has to be a way—"

As he ignored her, and refocused on the tangle ahead, she realized that if she made him halt just to have a conversation that went nowhere, she was only wasting the very thing she couldn't stand losing—like a plane crash survivor in the desert using the last of her water to wash her face instead of drink.

But goddamn it, when the hell was she going to make any forward progress here?

Finally, he slowed. Stopped.

"Get off," he said.

She was already on that, and she was also on the trigger to that collar—in the event this pre-dawn ride was merely an excuse to confirm her opinion about this damp, bug-ridden, leaf-choked place being where the bloated corpses of women were found. Or, in her case, females. Not that her remains would last long. Even with the canopy of vines and tree leaves overhead, the warning prickle on her skin told her that the sun was gathering momentum on its rise.

"We go on foot for the rest of the way."

Ahmare was grateful as he took off at a jog, that backpack of his strapped on so tight, it was like the saddle on a horse, nothing loose and slappy.

The way he held off branches and ducked and dodged was impressive, and she found herself mirroring his movements, the two of them becoming dance partners to the tune of such classics as "Up in Smoke in Ten More Minutes," "Where the Fuck Are We?" and the old standby "Jesus Christ, When Will We Get There."

And then everything became darker and a little cooler as they hit a gradual rise.

The vines backed off and the tree trunks grew smaller and the canopy lifted enough so she wasn't getting smacked in the face. Underfoot, there were rotting layers of decomposing leaves, a tiramisu of terrain.

Great, they'd gotten through the salad course. Now they were on to dessert.

Rocks now. Granite outcroppings with crevasses.

They were skirting the base of a mountain, cool air coming down from a summit that she could not see, the rivers of temperature change so distinct, she knew exactly when she entered and left them.

The prisoner stopped next to a rotting stump.

Picking up two sticks, each about three feet in length, he laid one next to the other at an angle.

"What are you doing?" she demanded, looking up through the trees.

She blinked hard at the shockingly pale sky, her retinas yelling at her.

"Come on, this way."

When she didn't jump back into the run, he grabbed her hand and dragged her along as her eyes watered and her sight was limited to mostly blurry what-is-that.

The prisoner jerked her to a halt. "Squeeze through here."

Trying to focus, she wondered what the hell he was talking about. There was no "here" that she could see, just a collection of massive boulders that seemed to have been dropped like balls from the hand of a god at the foot of the mountain they were going around.

"Here."

He changed her angle, pulling her around to reveal . . . yes, there was a slice of a gap in there.

Ahmare went think-thin sideways, her windbreaker scraping the lichen on both front and back. Soon enough, the compression gave way to a larger hidden belly illuminated only by the fissure she'd gone through. When the prisoner joined her, she was so close to him, she got his hair in her face.

Click.

The flashlight he outed beamed around. "Just where I remembered."

She had no clue what he was talking about. There was only more of the blackened rock wall of the narrow cave—

The prisoner reached up and dropped a camouflage drape that had been hooked into the stone, the heavy-duty fabric painted and stitched to disguise its true, man-made identity. Behind the folds, a stainless steel door streaked with the earthy blood of the forest gleamed like a mud puddle.

The prisoner punched something into a keypad mounted on the left side at waist height. There was no series of beeps. Nothing lit up. Nothing released, either.

"Damn it." He repeated the sequence. "Come on—"

Like a sleeper who'd hit the snooze button, some kind of system woke up and there was a dull *thunk* followed by a slide that resonated too loudly for there to be much grease on whatever was moving.

The hiss was less air lock, more not-been-opened-in-twenty-years.

As Duran went in first, Ahmare wanted to be flashlighting things, but she had his trigger box in one hand and a gun in the other.

There was no telling what was in there, and she was taking no damned chances.

12

EXACTLY AS HE'D LEFT it, Duran thought as he stepped inside the bunker and motion-activated lighting came on.

The hideaway was a stainless steel room set into the base of the mountain, a proverbial bread box buried in the earth. He'd built and outfitted the place over the period of a year and a half, and the hideout had been crucial for his revenge plan. He'd stolen money from the cult's vast resources to have it constructed, siphoning cash out of the cult's vault and then paying humans, who had no idea they were working for a vampire, to complete the project. The electricity that fed it had likewise been purloined from the spiritual compound, miles of cable buried underground.

Ahmare entered with her gun up and her thumb on his collar's trigger.

As she looked around, he measured the twenty-by-twenty space with the eye of a host and found the single bunk, rudimentary toilet stall, and bare metal floor wanting only in ways that didn't matter.

Who the hell cared if you had something soft to lie on? This place was a catch-your-breath-on-the-escape salvation.

Or, in their case, a wait-out-the-day launchpad.

Duran leaned back out and reattached the camouflage drape on the hooks. Then he shut the vault door and entered the lock code. The good news was there was no other way in. The bad news was there was no other way out. Hopefully, Chalen's guards had had to back off because of the approaching sun. He did not want the conqueror knowing about this cave.

"Shit," he muttered.

The female wheeled around, her ponytail swinging in a wide arc behind her head. "What?"

"I meant to get a pair of scissors from Nexi." He took off his backpack and scratched his beard. "I have to lose all this hair before we infiltrate." When she just stared at him, he frowned. "What."

"I guess you are really taking me there."

"Yes, I am." He sat down on the floor, crossing his legs. "Let's food up and get some sleep. Soon as night falls, it's going to be nonstop until you either get what Chalen wants or you die trying."

As she joined him, she put her gun away, but kept that trigger in her hand.

"You can relax." He took the sandwiches she and Nexi had made out of the backpack. "If I were going to hurt you, I wouldn't be handing you calories."

"How far away are we?" she asked as she accepted what he held out—and kept that trigger on her thigh. "How much more do we have to travel."

Frustration that had nothing to do with her made him want to argue the point that he wasn't going to get aggressive on her. He started eating to keep himself from wasting hot air.

"Not all that far."

"How far."

As she stared at him, he knew it was a fair question. Hell, after what he'd seen and experienced in the cult, he knew all too well the dangers that came with putting your life in the hands of another. And he was tempted to tell her everything: the location of the hidden entrance to the cult's underground facility, the plan for after they'd breached the security system, where Chalen's beloved was kept, and how to work the evac.

There were two problems with full disclosure. One, it had been twenty years, and although he knew the cult was still going strong—because the *Dhavos* had relished his role as a demigod too goddamn much to ever give it up—there was no knowing what had changed since Duran had last been there. What intel he had could be obsolete, and without him to figure things out? She was going to fail spectacularly.

The second reason he kept quiet? He had to remain indispensable or he lost his only leverage with her. There was going to come a moment when he was going to need to go his own way, when their objectives of infiltrating the compound and evading capture were going to shift to separate imperatives.

When her goal to get the beloved and his only chance for revenge were going to take them in different directions.

There was no telling when this split was going

to occur, and because of the way Chalen had set this up, she was supposed to bring Duran back to that cell in the conqueror's dungeon. Not going to happen. And he had to make sure she was placed in the position of having to choose between her brother's life and his own freedom.

It was his only chance.

As the grim reality of their "relationship" resonated with him, he thought it was ironic that his version of freedom was about killing another. It wasn't a safe home, a mate, or even an absence of physical pain.

Freedom was murdering his father for everything that had been done to his *mahmen*. And then, if he lived through that?

He was going to return to Chalen's castle. But not as a prisoner.

So no, he could not provide her with more information.

Abruptly, Duran's eyes lowered to her mouth—and a thought that was truly, fundamentally, incredibly unhelpful ricocheted like a stray bullet through his head: He wished he could provide her with other things.

Like his blood . . . his sex.

That he went to such an inappropriate place,

even if it was only in his mind, made him recall when her scent had first registered. There was something about this particular female that kindled him, and he couldn't explain it. Back when he'd been in the cult, there had been no sex allowed—at least not unless the *Dhavos* decreed it, and then it involved the great male himself.

Duran had always been too worried about rescuing his *mahmen* to think much about the ban or to follow through on whatever might have, ever so briefly, turned his eye. And then when he'd been in the dungeon? Taking those veins had been about survival, not attraction.

This female . . . Ahmare . . . had changed all that for him. Not that either one of them were in a position to do anything about it. Or, in her case, so inclined.

"Water?" he asked as he held out a jug.

This had to be what canned corn felt like, Ahmare thought as she chewed and looked around at all the metal.

The bunker had been fabricated from sheets of steel bolted together, the seams overlapping and riveted with vertical lineups of bolts. For some reason, the orderly rows of hexagonal heads made her think of the old Victorian dresses that had been in her *mahmen*'s closet, the buttons down the backs evenly spaced in their hooks or holes like well-behaved pupils.

Taking another bite of the sandwich she'd made with the Shadow, she found the bread and salami all texture, no taste in her mouth. But it wasn't like she was eating to enjoy.

"More water?" the prisoner said.

As she took what he held out and drank again, a part of her brain acknowledged that she was placing her lips where his had been.

Her eyes went to his beard. She could see nothing of his mouth with the long growth and she decided that was a good thing. Unless, of course, everything under there was ugly, then maybe it would help—because she shouldn't be thinking about things like lips . . . and tongues.

His lips. His tongue.

The trouble was, his scent in her nose, replacing as it did the tinny high notes of the metal-laced air, was working telephone lines on her switchboard that hadn't rung in a very, very long time.

And then there were his shoulders. Under the well-washed flak shirt he'd put on, they shifted as he took his bites, unbaggied a second sandwich, drank more water. Every time his arm rose, his bicep pulled the sleeve so tight she knew its seam was straining, and every time his arm went down, the shirt seemed to breathe a sigh of relief, a test passed.

His hair was drying now that they were out of the humidity, the waves turning into curls at the long ends, and she had a feeling it would be soft to the touch in a way his body would not. The shampoo he'd used in the Shadow's shower had left it all shiny—or maybe it had just been soap that he'd rubbed all over his head.

Funny, she couldn't smell whatever it had been. Usually at the gym where she worked, she had to train her nose away from all the bodywashes, Biolages, and colognes, the human need to artificially enhance their scents a reflection of their subpar olfactory range.

She had this male in her nose and down the back of her throat—

Stay focused on Ahlan, she told herself. What she needed to do was—

"I'm not going to hurt you."

As the prisoner spoke, Ahmare jerked and had to catch up with what the syllables meant.

"You're staring at me," he said as he finished the sandwich. "And I can only guess you're worried about how the day is going to go. So let me just get that out of the way. I'm not going to touch you."

The fact that her libido felt a sting of rejection made her want to bang her head into one of the walls until she left a dent in the shape of her own face.

He pointed over to the bunk. "You can sleep there." Then he pointed across the way in the opposite direction, to a bare wall. "I'll sleep here. And you always have that trigger. You can drop me in a heartbeat, isn't that what you said?"

Yes, she had been reminding herself of that fact at different points in this shitty adventure they were on. But concern for her personal safety hadn't been why she'd been staring at him now, not that he was ever going to know the real reason.

"So tell me about your brother," the prisoner said as he packed up the empty baggies, picking one to hold all the others.

Ahmare took a deep breath and figured talking was better than silence. "He's about six-five, so a little shorter than you. Dark hair like mine. Eyes my green color. He came along sixty years after me. I was excited."

Such basic statistics. That told nothing about Ahlan, really.

She stared down at the half-moon that she'd made in the bread when she'd taken her bite. "Live wire, Ahlan was—I mean, Ahlan *is*—a live wire. And that was a great characteristic before the raids, something that made the house come alive. After my parents were killed, though . . ." She shook her head. "He went off the rails. In that regard, we both played to type. I doubled down on the self-control, he became a firework going in a thousand different directions. I refused to think about my grief, burying myself in learning skills in self-defense and weapons that came too late. He ran from his, following any distraction he could."

Clearing her throat, she looked up. "I can't finish this sandwich. Do you want it?"

The prisoner reached out, and it was then that she noticed two out of his five fingers had no nails.

"They pulled them off so many times," he explained, "that they stopped growing back."

"I'm sorry," she whispered as he popped what she'd given him into his mouth and put his hand palm up in his lap so the nail beds didn't show.

"How did Chalen get involved in the story?" he asked.

She opened her mouth to speak. But couldn't seem to get any words out.

The prisoner's brows went low, but he didn't seem offended. It was more like bad memories were coming back to him.

"My father gave me to Chalen," he told her. When she recoiled, he smiled. At least she thought he did. It was hard to be sure because of the beard. "My father is a very superstitious male, and superstition becomes a hard fact if you believe in it enough."

"I don't understand."

"My father believes that if you kill a direct descendant of yours, you suffer a mortal event yourself. It's like in his mind, he and I are intrinsically tied together, and if he causes my death, it's tantamount to committing suicide. He'll die as well."

"I've never heard of anything like that."

"It's an Old Country thing."

"I was born in the New World."

"So was I. The old ways live on, though, don't they." He planted his palms flat behind his hips and leaned into them. "He also believed I was going to come after him one night. Tricky situation for a guy who has plans to live a long life. His personal Grim Reaper out in the world, tracking him, waiting for him to slip up, and yet he couldn't eliminate the threat."

"You make it sound like you're his killer."

"I will be."

Ahmare blinked at this. "Why?"

"He raped my *mahmen*. Repeatedly. That's how I was born. He had her once and couldn't stop. When her needing came, he took her over and over again. The nature of his addiction to her crippled him, and I believe his plan was to kill her as soon as he had his last hurrah during her fertile time—like a goddamn alcoholic going on a bender. But then when it was over, it dawned on him that he might get in trouble with that whole can't-kill-my-young thing. He had to wait to see if it took, if she got pregnant, and she did. I have no doubt he hoped she and I would both die on the birthing bed because I heard he had repeated nightmares that what he had sired would exact revenge for the way the conception had happened. No such luck on the maternal/fetal funeral, and then, horror of horrors, I was a son. Like a female wouldn't be strong enough to take revenge?"

"So he gave you to Chalen so someone else would kill you."

"Bingo."

"You were a member of the cult, then?"

"I was born into it, yes."

"And what happened to your *mahmen*?"

"My father kept her alive because he was in love with her and he liked to torture her with his presence. The second she died of natural causes, he sent me to Chalen. He might have done that sooner, but I look like him, and every time she met my eyes, it was like he was right with her. He's a sick fuck." There was a long pause. "She loved me, though." As the prisoner's voice cracked, he cleared his throat. "I don't know how . . . but she loved me as her son. How the hell could she do that? She should have hated me."

"None of this was your fault."

Bleak eyes met her own. "No, I'm just the living, breathing symbol of everything she endured. I wouldn't have been able to be like her if the roles had been reversed."

"A *mahmen*'s love is the greatest force in the universe." Ahmare thought of her own family. "It is sacred. It's stronger than hate. Stronger than death, too. Sometimes, I wake up in the middle of the day and I can swear my *mahmen*'s hand is on my shoulder and her sweet voice is telling me all will be well because she will never leave me. It's as though, even from the Fade, she watches over me."

But if that was true, Ahmare thought, how had her brother gone down such a bad path? Surely the female watched over him, too?

"I will never understand it," the prisoner said.

She refocused. "You don't have to. You don't even need to accept it because every breath you take and each beat of your heart does that. Your sire might have been evil, but love won in the end, didn't it?"

There was another long period of quiet.

"No," he said eventually. "I don't think it does."

13

———•••———

S O HOW GOOD ARE you with a knife?"

As the prisoner asked the question, Ahmare had a quick image of her stab—*har-har*—at decapitation.

"Average," she said as her stomach rolled. "Why?"

"I need to get this off." He tugged at his beard and hair. "And without scissors and a razor, I'm going to need help."

"Mirror," she added.

"Huh?"

"You'd also do well to have a mirror." She shifted onto her knees and unholstered her hunting knife. "But I can do it. My father used to shave with a straight edge and he taught me how."

"You mind if we go over there?" Duran nodded at the bunk. "I'm aching."

As he got his height and weight off the floor, he grunted and there were cracking sounds, like branches snapping during the dry fall. Also a pop or two that made her wonder if he wasn't going to need to have a bone set.

"How old are you?" she blurted.

"I don't keep track of those things. But I am certainly too young to be moving like this." He limped over and groaned as he sat himself down on the thin, bare mattress. "Too many broken things healed in bad ways."

Ahmare took her time getting to her feet. Otherwise, it felt like she was showing off the fact that she didn't hurt all over.

As she approached him with the knife, she was amazed that he sat there so calmly as someone he didn't know came toward him with a shiny blade capable of doing damage—

Without warning, the Mississippi delta of blood spilling from Rollie's open, ragged neck barged in, an out-of-order interloper that she would rather have stayed away from her proverbial establishment. God, if she never thought about that death again, it would be too soon. The trouble was, she couldn't ignore the fact that the last time she had had this hilt in her palm, it had been to kill.

Now, it was to shave.

Could she be like the blade? she wondered. Could she turn away from carnage and return to the mundane? Along those lines, after all this, what would she be like, if she survived?

She thought of that hand analogy that she'd given the Shadow, the one where Rollie's dead fingers penetrated the big divide in her life and contaminated her peaceable past. Except maybe the contamination hadn't started with Rollie. Maybe it had started with the raids, with the death of her parents. Maybe that was the beginning of everything turning toxic and her present circumstance was a trickle-down of her parents' blood being spilled.

Maybe she'd gotten the timeline wrong, even if her conclusion was right.

"Well?" the prisoner prompted.

She had come to stand before him, she realized, and she was staring down at his bearded face without seeing him.

"Sorry," she said as she put the trigger in her back pocket and tried to focus on how she was going to get rid of that facial hair without cutting him.

When he reached out and took her hand, she jumped, but all he did was hold on to her, a solid, surprisingly calm anchor amidst the chaos.

"It's okay." His voice was soft. "I know what it's like to have the world disappear behind things you'd rather not re-see. You can take your time coming back, and not just because we've got hours ahead of us."

Ahmare looked down at where they had unexpectedly connected. His palm dwarfed hers, but the warmth of his skin was exactly the same as her own.

His thumb, his nail-less, bruised thumb, stroked over her twice.

Then he dropped his hold and tilted his chin up, ready whenever she was.

Tears formed in Ahmare's eyes, making him wavy. She could handle anything but kindness, she realized.

The female was absolutely stunning, Duran thought. And not in the conventional sense.

It wasn't even about her physical presence. In fact, as the conviction overtook him, he couldn't have described any of her features. He couldn't even see her.

Because it wasn't about her face or her body.

Ahmare was beautiful to him because of the way she made him feel. She was like a stroke of luck when nothing had been breaking your way or the unexpected relief of a weight that had been crushing you . . . or the rescue boat that appeared just as your head was going under after your very last gasp.

And in response, for the first time in a very long while—maybe ever—he felt something loosen in his gut. It took him a minute to figure out what it was.

Safety. He felt safe with her—and wasn't that ironic, given that she had a nine-inch hunting knife in her hand. But the thing was, he knew she wasn't going to come after him, and not just because she needed him to take her to the beloved. Cruelty was just not part of her nature. Like the color of her eyes and the shape of her body, the fact that she was a defender, a peacemaker instead of an aggressor, was an intrinsic part of her.

"I'll start with the beard."

It took him a second to figure out what she was talking about. Oh, right. The shave and two bits.

She gathered the growth off his chin at its lowest point. "I'm going to try to be as gentle as I can, okay? Let me know if I hurt you."

He hadn't heard that in a while, he thought.

There was a pull, and he tightened the muscles in his neck to keep his head in place. And then she started to slice.

"It's dull," she muttered. "Damn it, I'm sorry."

"It's okay. Do what you have to."

Do what you want to, he added to himself. He kept that quiet, though, because suddenly he wasn't thinking about the beard, the knife, the shave. He was thinking about other things, other situations.

When he might encourage her. Might ask things of her. Might . . . beg things of her.

His eyes locked on her mouth. Her concentration was such that she had taken her lower lip between her teeth on one side, her sharp canine pressing into the soft pink flesh. Down between his legs, behind the zipper fly of the combat pants, he felt his sex thicken. The response, though natural, seemed a mark of disrespect, but there was no apologizing for it—not without forcing her to acknowledge something that she no doubt would have been put off by.

Unfortunately, there was no cutting off the erection, either. The fact that his cock got strangled by the seam of the pants seemed a fitting punishment, however, and he hoped the discomfort might lead to a deflation, the big guy forced to get back in line—

A sudden release of pressure made his head flip back, and he had to catch himself on the bunk. Glancing down, he measured how much she had taken off of his beard. Six inches. Minimum.

Just think, the very ends of all that had sprouted from his face after his last shave. The one he had done on himself without having any idea that in fifteen minutes he would be struck on the back of his head and then wake up in a living nightmare that would last twenty years.

The one that he had taken special care with because he had wanted to be clean-cut for his *mahmen*'s Fade ceremony.

He should have known, however, that with her death, his fortunes were going to get worse.

"I was too clouded by grief."

"What?" Ahmare said as she came back at him with the blade.

There was a tug off to the side as she isolated a section that was closer to his jawline. When that was cut, she moved over a little. And again. Again. Again. Until what she was putting down on the mattress was tufts instead of a single, cohesive length.

"I should have known what my father was going to do," he heard himself say. "I should have seen it coming. But I was too broken by her passing." He closed his eyes as he remembered the decline that had led up to the death. "There had been something wrong with her stomach. She had stopped eating about a month before. If she'd been human, I would have said she had the cancer, but in any event, something wasn't working right and there was no way to get her to a healer. In those last weeks, as she grew weaker and weaker, she didn't even take from my father when he insisted on offering her his vein. I had been so proud of her because denying him made him insane, but I didn't know she was sick. I would have chosen the humiliation and impotent rage I always felt when she took from him if it had meant she'd have stayed with me."

Abruptly, he popped his lids open. "But that's

selfish, right? I mean, to want her to live no matter what it cost us both just so I don't have to mourn."

"That's normal." The female met his eyes. "It sounds like all you had was each other."

"I think I wanted her to see me get my revenge. She wouldn't have liked that, though. She was like you."

"Me?" Dark brows lifted. "Here, tilt this way."

He obliged, letting his head fall away from her gentle urging. Then again, he had a feeling if she'd asked him to cut off his own hand, he would have done so—and then made sure to clean her blade off before he returned it to her.

"She was a good soul," he said. "A kind person. She didn't want to do harm. Just like you."

Ahmare laughed in a harsh way. "I spend my nights teaching self-defense. It's all about punches and kicks, target practice and technique."

"So innocent people don't get hurt."

"I suppose I've never thought of it that way." She eased back and assessed her work. "Other side. And stay really still. I'm getting close to your skin—I wish we had shaving cream to soften things up."

"There's running water in that sink. And a bar of soap. Or at least that's how I left this place when I built it."

She lowered the blade. "You did all this?"

Duran looked around. "It was part of my grand scheme, and now just a relic to the best laid plans. My *mahmen* used to help me sneak out of our room. Every time she created a diversion and I went into air ducts, I know she hoped I would escape and never come back. My idea was to get her out, leave her here, and return for her after I was done with killing my father. Not the way any of it went."

He frowned and focused properly on Ahmare. "You know . . . I never expected to tell anyone all of this."

"Because it's private?"

Duran looked away. "Something like that."

In fact, he'd assumed the only person he'd ever open up to was his *mahmen* when they were reunited in the Fade—after he'd found some way of dying without committing suicide as soon as he killed his father.

That had been his ultimate endgame, that loophole in the whole if-you-kill-yourself-you-can't-get-into-the-Fade thing.

Then again, maybe all that afterlife stuff was just like his father's belief that you couldn't cause the death of your own young and live on. Maybe it was just superstition. In any event, given what he had learned of mortal existence—and this was even before Chalen had gotten his claws into him—skipping his mortal due on earth for an eternity with the only loved one he'd ever had had seemed like a no-brainer.

But now . . . as he looked into this female's eyes, he could sense himself making a shift on that one.

Ahmare kind of made him want to stick around. Even though that was crazy talk.

14

---·—·—·—·---

THE SOAP AND WATER were a godsend, Ahmare decided. Without them, she would
have turned Duran's face into a Halloween
mask.

"Okay, I think we're done."

She eased back—and could not look away from
what she had revealed. During the shaving, she had
been paying so much attention to not cutting him
that she'd gotten no impression of his face. Now,

with the overgrowth gone, it was as if she were meeting him for the first time.

He had hollows in his cheeks and his jawline was too sharp. Eyes that had been calculating and aggressive now seemed wary.

The lips were even better than she'd imagined.

"That bad, huh," he muttered as he put the bowl of soapy water and the cloth she'd used aside.

Ahmare wanted to tell him that, on the contrary, he was attractive. Very attractive. Beautiful, in a word. But some things were better left unsaid.

Would that they had remained unthought.

"Will you shave my head, too?" he asked.

"Oh, God . . . not the hair."

"I don't have lice, you know."

At that, he reached across his chest and scratched the outside of his opposite arm. Bug bite, probably. She had them, too, but at least she knew they didn't have any ticks. After their barrel-ass through the brush, if they'd been human, they would have been covered with those carriers of Lyme disease, but vampire blood beat deet any night of the week when it came to that particular variety of bloodsuckers, a professional courtesy extended in both directions that unfortunately didn't apply to mosquitoes.

"Your hair is . . ." She wiped her mouth for no reason. "Well, it's . . . too beautiful to cut."

Shit. Had she just shared with him That Which Should Not Be Spoken?

Yup, going by his shocked expression, she had.

Duran *was* beautiful all over, though, in the way only a survivor could be. He had been through such cruelty, the road map of salted scars on his skin the kind of thing that told her way too much of what had been done to him. And the fact that he had somehow been strong enough to endure and not come out the other side insane, mean, or a vegetable, made him stronger than anyone she had ever met.

God, those humans in those gyms—hefting weights, worrying about whey protein, and posing in front of a fan base that lived and cheered only inside their own heads—were CGIs of strength compared to this male.

And yet as powerful as Duran's inner core was—and she wasn't talking about his abs—here he was sitting in front of her, staring up at her with a shyness that suggested, however nuts it seemed, that he cared what she thought he looked like.

That her opinion mattered.

That he wanted her to like him. Be attracted to him. Be captivated a little, in spite of their crazy circumstances.

"I am," she whispered.

"You are . . . what?"

"Attracted to you." She cleared her throat. "That's what you're wondering right now, aren't you."

His eyes shifted away so fast, he had to catch himself on the edge of the bunk. "How did you know."

"It's okay."

"No, it isn't."

"Well, don't pretend I didn't give you the answer you wanted." She had no idea where her brass balls came from. Probably because she had nothing to lose. "I'm glad, actually."

"You don't seem petty enough to care what your wingman looks like."

"It's just good to know I can still feel this way." As his stare came back to her, she shrugged. "It's been forever. I thought . . . I guess, I thought sex wasn't going to be a part of my life anymore. That the raids and losing my parents and my old life had taken that side of me away. It's nice to know that's not true—"

"It's not right."

She took a step back from him and cleared her throat. "Sorry. Guess I misread things."

"No, not that." He shook his head. "It's just a complication that isn't going to help you or me."

"Agreed. But I don't expect anything from you, you know."

He shifted himself away from her, planting the soles of his boots on the bare metal floor. And as he stood up, he moved slowly, something she assumed was because of his soreness. But then . . .

There was a hard ridge at the front of his hips. A thick, hard ridge that distended the fly of his combats.

"My apologies," he said roughly. "I can't do anything about it other than promise you I'm not going there. I told you I wouldn't hurt you, and I mean it."

As if sex with him couldn't be anything other than painful for her.

As if he were dirty.

Ahmare thought about the time they had here in the bunker, the hours they were going to have to spend trapped together in this stainless steel wayside mission that sheltered them from the sun.

It was mysterious who a person wanted. And only sometimes did it make sense.

"The hair can wait," he said gruffly. "Let's just try and get some sleep. Like I told you, you get the bunk, I'll take the floor. Not that there's much difference to them."

15

———◆◆◆———

TWILIGHT IN A MAN-MADE universe.

Duran played God in their stainless steel world, lowering the lights, the glow off all the metal a false gloaming. In the near darkness, he sat on the floor across from the bunk Ahmare was on, his back against the wall, his legs out in front of him. He tried not to listen to her breathing. Dwell on her scent. Hear the rustle as she took off her windbreaker and used it as a pillow.

He should have thought to bring a blanket for her.

As time began to crawl by and the silence thickened to hair shirt proportions, the lack of illumination amplified his senses and his absorption in her. But he wasn't sure that wouldn't have happened anyway.

More shuffling, and thanks to his peripheral vision, he could tell she was facing him now. He didn't trust himself to look right at her. If he did, he might be tempted to get up, walk over, and give her something softer to lie on.

Something naked to lie on.

"How did you get the name Duran?" she asked.

He closed his eyes and savored his name on her lips. It made him feel blessed in some way . . . anointed.

Okay, that was crazy. But the trouble was, in this quiet, dim space, his emotions toward this female were as expansive as his senses, and everything about this time with her was like a horizon, a vast sky under which he could travel, safe from foul weather and sheltered from all harm, back to a home he'd never had.

Back to her, even though she was neither a destination nor anywhere he'd ever been before.

It was all a falsehood, he told himself, created by the chemistry between them. Except . . . sometimes when you felt things deeply enough, the strength of the delusions was such that reality could get re-wired, at least temporarily. He knew this because of what he'd seen in the cult. He'd witnessed first-hand what devotion did to people, watched it turn a corrupt mortal into a savior in the eyes of lost souls who were willing to surrender every part of them-selves to another.

He had always vowed such a thing would never happen to him.

"It doesn't matter," he muttered, answering her question about his name.

"So it came from your father?"

"He insists people call me by it, yes."

She was frowning, he thought without looking at her. He could sense her thinking things over.

"Can I ask you something?" she said.

"You just did."

"Who is your father, exactly."

"It doesn't matter—"

"He's the *Dhavos*, isn't he."

Duran stretched his arms overhead and cracked his back. In any other circumstance, he would have avoided the question—by leaving the room, if he had to. No such luck on that one.

"Yes," he said after a while. "He is. His name is Excalduran."

As she exhaled, the way her breath left her, long and slow and low, was an I'm-sorry that he appreciated she didn't put into words.

"So it's eight in the morning," she murmured.

Duran frowned. "Really?"

"You know," she continued, "I've been lying to myself. In my head, I've been saying that we'll be here twelve hours. That's all I've been willing to grant the daylight. But with it being summer? Fifteen, I figure. At least."

"The time will pass quickly."

It already had. And God, he was glad she'd changed the subject.

She repositioned herself again. "Actually, it'll pass the same as it always does. The length of minutes doesn't change, and neither does the number of them required to make up an hour. But man, it feels like forever."

"This is true."

He didn't know what the hell he was saying. The sound of her voice was a caress against his body, and he was thickening again. Hardening again. For someone who had never had to worry about that kind of shit, he had fresh insight into the inconveniences of the male sex.

"Your scent has changed," she said in a lower voice.

Duran closed his eyes and banged the back of his head into the smooth wall. "Sorry."

"Don't be."

"We should go to sleep." Great suggestion. Yup. "It will—"

"I'm not a virgin."

His mouth fell open. And then he considered the idea of her with another male, any other male. As jealousy heated his blood for absolutely no good reason, he redirected himself by thinking about Chalen's guards.

"Neither am I," he said tightly.

"Have you ever been mated? Do you have a *shellan*?"

"No."

"Good. I don't have to feel guilty then. I'm single, too, by the way. Before the raids, there was a male or two, but no one serious. No one I brought home to my parents."

Duran put his hands up to his face and scrubbed.

"It's sad," she continued, "that they'll never meet any young I might have. Any *hellren* I may take."

"I'm glad."

"Excuse me?" she said sharply.

"No, no." He dropped his hands. "I didn't mean it like that. I'm glad that you're thinking like there's something on the other side of this. That your life continues. It's a good thing to focus on a happy future."

"I wouldn't go that far," she said.

You're still way ahead of me, he thought.

That was why he wasn't crossing the distance between them. No matter how open she seemed and how much he wanted her, he wasn't going to do to her on purpose what he'd done to Nexi by mistake.

One goal. He had one goal. After which, like a fuse having done its job to set off a bomb, he would cease to exist.

Literally.

16

AHMARE HAD MEANT WHAT she'd said about time. It was true that seconds and minutes and hours were fundamentals, unchanging in spite of your perception. But damn, in this silent, darkened bunker, sheltered by the dirt skirt of a mountain, she and the prisoner had tapped into infinity.

Duran, that was.

She and *Duran* had entered a strange kind of forever, sure as if all of time was a serene, temperate pond so perfectly calibrated to their body temperature and utterly, completely still that they had been unaware of all the wading steps they'd taken to this submersion. In fact, the illusion of infinity was so complete that even her brother's reality had lost some of its sting. It wasn't that she had forgotten Ahlan's situation; it was more like that sense of urgency she'd been motivated by had run itself out on the racetrack of her fight-or-flight response and was taking a breather on a bench off to the side, gulping water and panting as it prepared for the next relay.

Her panic would be back the second it was safely dark outside.

And in its place, a different urge was consuming her.

Across the way, Duran's body was giving off all kinds of arousal signals: Those dark spices, for one. For another, he was moving around a lot, his boots squeaking as he crossed and recrossed his legs, his throat clearing, his shoulder cracking as he stretched again. And again. And . . . again.

She knew exactly the kind of ants that were under his skin. The tingle in the spine. The flush of heat in the vein that flowed but did not ebb.

She had been hoping he would act on their sexual tension first, and that was some cowardly stuff right there. Such a lame move, as if she didn't have to be responsible for her own choice if he was the one to cross over and kiss her first: Like if it happened that way, she didn't have to feel guilty that her brother was suffering and she was getting off with a stranger.

Closing her eyes, she crossed her arms over her chest and resolved to cut the crap and go to sleep.

Two seconds later, she was sitting up. Putting her weight on her feet. Going to him.

Being the one who forged the trail across the vacant yet somehow utterly cluttered space between them. And just as time had become distorted, so, too, did distance—miles, she walked miles over the course of the fifteen or so feet that separated them.

Duran cursed in a low mutter as she stopped in front of him.

"You can tell me no," she said, "but I'm not going to apologize."

"I don't know what that word means right now."

"Which one?"

"The one that matters."

Lowering herself down, she straddled his outstretched legs, staying on her knees. Her hands went to his shirt, finding the soft fabric, pressing into the hard chest underneath. When she leaned forward, she tilted her head to one side and hesitated.

He seemed frozen. Incapable of response. Shocked, as if he didn't know what to expect. He wasn't pushing her away, though. Far from it. And those dark spices were a roar in her nose now, a dense erotic scent that intoxicated her even further.

As his lips parted, he swallowed hard. "Please . . ." he whispered. "Do it."

Ahmare lowered her mouth to his. With his level of arousal, she thought he'd grab her by the back of the neck and go hard-grind with the kiss. Instead, he closed his eyes as she brushed against him softly, and beneath her mouth, his lips trembled—until she captured them fully, that was. Then he responded, mirroring her motions, the caressing, the stroking, the plying.

When she entered him with her tongue, he gasped. Groaned. Jerked his hips.

Underneath her, his body was live-wire tight, his palms braced against the floor, his arms shaking as he held himself in place, his leg muscles contracting in a series of spasms. She appreciated the restraint, she truly did.

It meant he respected her in that old school way.

But it was not what she wanted.

Breaking from the kiss, she sat back on his knees and knew she had to do something to get him into gear. The kissing was nice, the kissing was great, but the prelude was not the purpose of this, and he seemed unwilling to be the one to take things to the next level.

Pulling the bottom of her shirt out from the waistband of her pants, she had a stupid thought about how Under Armour had made this thin, long-sleeved body upholstery to "wick sweat" and "cool as it covered" during workouts. Good attributes if you were in the gym or on a run.

Totally irrelevant in this particular hot-and-bothered situation.

Worse than irrelevant.

An impediment.

Duran's eyes burned as she gripped the mesh, and he breathed like he had a car in each hand and was doing bicep curls. What she was about to show him seemed, given his rapt attention, like the kind of thing he needed to see more than he worried about oxygen.

Funny, how a male could tell you you were beautiful without saying a word.

Ahmare lifted the shirt slowly, not because she

wanted to artificially delay things or was having second thoughts. She wanted to savor the moment of revelation.

Except the sports bra underneath was something she'd forgotten about.

As she up-and-over'd the shirt, tossing it somewhere, she didn't care, she had meant to show him her breasts. Instead, hello, Champion.

Duran didn't seem to notice. He traced the wide straps and tight panel with his hot eyes, as if he were imagining the flesh underneath.

"Take it off for me," she said in a throaty voice.

More with the trembling on his side, but he didn't disobey the command. Hooking his thumbs under the lower edge of the wide band, he took the tight nylon upward—

Her breasts popped free, bouncing, the nipples tight and tingling thanks to the fabric's hard stroke.

Duran didn't get any further than that. He bailed on the removal job with the sports bra wedged under her armpits, her breasts compressed on top, extra full on the bottom. Sitting up, he put his mouth to her, sucking one of her nipples in, lapping at her with his warm, wet tongue.

Ahmare let her head fall back, and he caught her torso with a strong arm. Spearing into all that long hair of his, she moaned at the sweet tugging, the slip and slide and recapture, the switch to the other side. And even though the contact was only in one place, she felt it everywhere, all over her skin and throughout her body.

Especially between her legs.

Back with the kissing now, and positions were changing. He was moving them, shifting her as if she weighed nothing, laying her back against the hard floor that could have been a down mattress for all she knew. As he lay on top of her, a strange, hypersensitive numbness came over her, and she welcomed it just as she welcomed his body, now flush against her own, her clothing, and all of his, a total frustration.

She solved that problem quick.

Peeling the sports bra all the way off, she went for the buttons of his flak shirt. Her fingers were sloppy as she worked her way down the lineup, and then she was parting the two halves, finding smooth skin and hard muscle and volcanic warmth underneath.

Pants were supposed to be next on both sides, but she stayed awhile where they were, like a mountain climber enjoying a keyhole view that was not to be missed even though the summit was where they were headed. He was so different than she, the pads of muscles and thick, heavy bones the kind of thing that made her feel feminine, especially as her bare nipples met his torso.

The independent part of her, the fierce and strong part that had entered Chalen's castle without weapons, carrying the head of a dead man, rankled at the idea that somewhere in her was an unevolved female who wanted a male to chase her and catch her and hold her down while he entered her and bit her hard on the neck. While he marked her as his own. While he established a dominance that she was hot for. While he left his scent all over her.

Inside of her.

Yup, the modern side of her could do without those kind of he-man antics. But what was happening between them now wasn't modern; it was ancient. It was as old as the species itself. It was the basis of mortal existence, the door to immortality through the creation of a next generation.

Splitting her thighs, she pulled him even more fully on top of her, and Duran came readily, his body making its way between her legs, the ridge of his hard sex pushing into her core through their pants. As he started to roll into her and retreat, stroking them both, his hands, broad and warm and calloused, swept up to her breasts, learning her contours, caressing. Kissing deeply, they moved together, getting their rhythm down, a dress rehearsal for the naked penetration that was coming soon.

When she pushed her hands between them, he popped his hips up to create the space she needed to undo his fly, her fly. The shucking, inefficient and maddening, came next as they tried to keep kissing while kicking off everything south of the waist.

He had no underwear. Hers were no big deal.

And then they were fully naked.

Duran was magnificent skin to skin. And there were so many places to go with her hands and mouth . . .

But that would come later. First this essential union. Then the exploration.

17

DURAN HAD NEVER THOUGHT there could be anything more visceral, more consuming ... more important ... than revenge. Everything else he had ever experienced had been in the category of discardable distractions, the sights, smells, thoughts, or feelings like pennies spilled from his pockets, nothing valuable enough to make him stop and retrieve what he'd lost or ignored.

This, however ... *this* consumed him even more than his revenge.

Tasting Ahmare, feeling her skin against his, hearing her breath catch and then explode on an exhale, all of it was, for the first time since he had become aware of his father's cruelty and his *mahmen*'s suffering, a submersion of sense and sensation so complete that another need took the wheel of his intent and intentions and charted a course he was not going to argue with.

Hell, all he wanted to do was stomp on the gas.

And now was the moment.

As Ahmare tilted her hips and he felt the first brush of his erection over the hot core of her, he knew there was no going back.

Actually, that probably had been true the instant he had sensed her on the far side of the waterfall in his cell.

Some things were inevitable.

Some leaps were taken before you were aware of going over the edge.

Some songs called you too magically.

Except now, he fumbled. Everything leading up to this had been so smooth, as if they had done this a million times before even though it was a first for him on all accounts and obviously something fresh to her. But now he poked around, his cock's head swelling with every misguided almost-there, the half thrusts of his hips the kind of blind navigation that would get him where they needed him to be only by a stroke of luck.

Pun intended.

Ahmare solved this increasingly urgent problem by reaching between them, just as she had when she'd undone both of their pants. He gasped as her hand touched him, the bolt of electricity so great he saw stars and thought with horror that he'd orgasmed. But no. When the shock cleared, he was still hard and he hadn't left a mess all over her—

His body knew what do to.

As soon as she made the connection, something took over, his hips thrusting forward and driving him deep into her hold. Dimly, he was aware of a streak across his shoulders, her nails biting into him as she kicked her head back and arched up into his torso with a moan. Taking the back of her head in the palm of his hand so he didn't knock her out, he meant to go slow—and did nothing of the sort.

Pistoning against the cradle of her hips, he pounded into her, his lips peeling off his descended fangs, the need to bite her a not-right-now for two reasons: One, he hadn't asked, and she hadn't offered, but also because he'd have to slow down, maybe stop.

And that was impossible.

With every penetration and each retreat, he was building momentum and she was right there with him, matching his rhythm, mirroring his greed for more, faster, harder, *more*. Off in the distance, coming at him with lightning speed, was a terminal point of pleasure, and in the back of his mind, he remembered running out of Chalen's dungeon toward her car, an optical illusion making him believe the vehicle was rushing toward him instead of the other way around—

The intrusion of reality threatened to ground him, like a stake through his chest into the earth below, and he lost his step in the dance with Ahmare, his brain tripping him up, his rhythm off.

He shouldn't have worried, though.

All he had to do was look down into her eyes, her beautiful, shining eyes, and he was plugged right back into the moment.

She came as their stares found each other, and it was so incredible that this time he slowed because he was savoring the experience, not because he'd lost a connection to it. As pleasure came to her, her face contorted and her body stiffened, and around his erection, he felt her delicious hold tightening and releasing—

"Duran . . . oh, God, *Duran.*"

No one had ever said his name like that before. And he was captivated by the way she gasped and grabbed onto him, her breath seeming to freeze in her lungs. She was in heaven, and he knew he had put her there, and that was, even more than whatever his body was feeling, the very best part of what was an amazing experience.

He also had no intention of stopping.

As he rolled his hips and stroked her on the inside, she said his name again and moved her hands up to his shoulders, half-moons of sweet sting making him smile because he wanted her to draw blood from him. He wanted her to use him for her own pleasure for the rest of their lives, taking everything he had to give, accepting all parts of him.

As he continued to thrust, so she continued to orgasm. And he concentrated completely on what worked for her. What made her moan. How to go even deeper by gripping the back of one of her knees and cranking her leg up.

He didn't know what had given him the idea. But it was a stroke of genius going by the way she responded.

Duran knew when she was finally done because the tension left her completely and her hands slipped off his back, falling to the hard floor.

He stopped. And smiled at her exhaustion, peaceful as it was.

Except then she said, "What about you?"

Duran frowned as she focused her glassy eyes on him.

"We need to take care of you, too," she insisted, her words strung together as if she lacked the strength to differentiate the syllables.

When he still didn't respond, she reached up and stroked his face; then she lifted her head and pressed her lips to his. As her mouth clung to his, and then her tongue licked inside of him, his own needs rekindled and he realized she was right. He hadn't orgasmed. He was still rock hard inside of her.

"Come for me," she said into his mouth.

Then she worked herself against him, recreating the friction that had been the point of all of this. Closing his eyes, he concentrated on being inside of her, on everything that was so slick and tight, on the sensation of heat against heat.

Faster. Harder.

Faster . . .

. . . harder.

The endpoint she had reached refused to come to him, any orgasm stalling along its path toward him, the sensations getting just to the tipping point of release . . . but then going no further, like there was a barricade. Or a security checkpoint with an armed guard was more like it.

Sweat beaded his forehead, and he brushed the sting out of his eyes. Concentrating on where his arousal was and what it was doing and who to, he demanded that he get caught up again in the moment. Otherwise, he worried, she would find insult in what he could not control.

He tried another position, a different rhythm. He squeezed his eyes tight. He opened them to stare at her.

Eventually, he stopped, bracing an arm to hold himself off her. He was panting from exertion, not passion, as he tried to catch his breath.

"It's okay," she said as she ran a smoothing hand over the hot, steaming plane of his back. "Just let yourself go."

Closing his eyes, he gave it another shot, sure that this time would be different. This time, he'd be normal and do the normal thing, and then afterward they would hold each other and probably have two or three more sessions before the sun went down and they got back to reality. Teeth gritted, hips swinging, he bore down on his lower body like that would take care of the problem. Like he could force the orgasm out of himself, a cure for coital constipation.

All of the trying just seemed to be scaring off his goal.

No. Go.

Duran popped open his lids, ready to scream from frustration. He couldn't keep this up forever; he was going to hurt her and end up with a dislocated lower spine.

Maybe he'd just fake it. Except she'd know and that seemed even worse—

The solution presented itself as his eyes swung around and landed on an object that had fallen out of her pants.

As he reached for the trigger to his collar, he grabbed onto it like the lifesaver it was.

"Help me," he said. Begged was more like it.

Ahmare was confused—and then horrified as he put the black box into her palm.

"What? No, I'm not going to—"

Before she could argue, he pressed the button himself—

The electrical charge that went through him was

so powerful and sudden, he bit the inside of his mouth, tasting blood as his body went rigid from the shock. But goddamn it, the pain that lit up his skeleton, traveling down his spine and branching all the way to his fingers and toes, opened the door for his release. Like a crowd rushing a field, his orgasm exploded out of him, his erection kicking inside of Ahmare.

Losing himself in the sensations of pleasure and pain, he was blown apart even as he stayed whole, his brain incapable of processing anything other than what he had forced out of himself.

When he finally stilled, his head dropping to her shoulder, his breath sawing out of his open, bleeding mouth, he knew, without a doubt . . . that he had made the wrong call.

Ahmare was frozen under him, horrified.

The means had not been justified by the end, however huge the orgasm had been, and he sensed her withdrawal from him even as she lay beneath his tired, twitching body.

He didn't blame her.

18

WHEN NIGHTFALL FINALLY CAME, unhurried but on time, Ahmare was dressed and ready to go, standing in front of the way out, her weapons holstered around her body, her hair yanked back in a rubber band, her boots laced up and prepared to cover ground.

Behind her, on the far side of the partition that hid the toilet, Duran was emptying his bladder, something she had just done.

Odd, to feel like she was intruding on a private

moment of his given that she couldn't see around the partition, and hello—they'd had sex.

She closed her eyes and tried not to think of how it had ended. How they had awkwardly separated their bodies and then lain together on the cold, hard floor, the fit that had seemed so perfect, so seamless, now marked with knees and ribs, elbows and chins.

Are you okay?

Yes, are you?

She couldn't remember who had asked and who had answered. But she recalled returning to her bunk and him going back to his place on the floor across the way, their clothes hastily pulled on, Wite-Out to take care of a blunder at the typewriter.

Which blunder, though? Not the sex. She had no regrets there.

Are you okay?

Yes, are you?

Who had asked that first? Maybe it had been at the same time, and as for answers, were they both lying? She had been—she hadn't been okay and wasn't now—but the last thing she wanted was for him to feel compelled to take care of her.

As it was oh so very clear he was the one who needed to be looked after.

Maybe Duran was right. Maybe she was a healer at her core and so the idea that he'd had to hurt himself to orgasm made her heart ache.

Or perhaps her compassion was less to do with who she was than how she felt about him. Somehow, in the quiet moments in the bunker, she'd gotten attached to Duran, proof positive that emotional ties could strengthen in two ways: amount of time together or intensity of experience. And no one could argue they weren't in that second bucket of relationship building.

"You all set?"

When he spoke behind her, she jumped—like he might read her mind and know what she was thinking of. Covering her tracks, she made a show of turning around and facing him head-on, as if she didn't have things she wanted to hide from him, things like how she was worried about him. As well as sad, heartbreaking questions about what those guards might have done to him—

Oh, to hell with that, she *knew* what had been done to him. He'd told her he wasn't a virgin, and she feared that was only partially true. The wonder and surprise he'd shown when he'd entered her had clearly been because, at least in that way, it *had* been his first time.

Are you okay?

Yes, are you?

As their eyes met, everything about Duran was remote, his expression, his stare, even his big body, which somehow seemed totally self-contained. He'd cut off his hair—his lush, beautiful hair—in a series of hacks with her hunting knife, and she had to ignore the way the lengths lay on the floor like trash. Like they didn't matter. Like they hadn't been a part of him, grown from him and now ruined.

Then again, the circumstances under which—

"Are you ready," he prompted again.

She cleared her throat. "Yes, I am."

He nodded and entered a code on a panel. There was a hiss, and her nose tingled as the smell of the cave, of wet dirt and old mold, entered like it had wanted to come inside all along and conquer new, previously denied territory.

Ahmare went first without waiting for a plan from him. She just needed some fresh air, and she almost made it all the way through the tight-squeeze of the cave. Before she was out, though, Duran caught her by the shoulder, dropping his hold the second she stopped.

"I need to go first," he whispered. "If you get killed because Chalen's guards are waiting for us, or the *Dhavos* knows we're here, no one's saving your brother."

"And if you get killed, I have no clue where I'm going."

"I'm going first. Wait for my signal."

As he pushed past her and stepped out into the humid night, she stuck right on his heels, a gun in one hand, her knife in the other. That trigger box, which she now hated, was holstered at her waist. She'd thought about leaving it behind because she was not worried about him turning on her. Still, he might run off, or at least try to, although she didn't want to think about dropping him to the ground just to keep him with her—

Duran stopped short and glared at her. "What the hell are you doing?"

Even though he was talking softly, his expression put plenty of volume in his words.

"I'm not getting left behind."

He pointed over her shoulder. "Get back in there."

"No." She met him right in the angry eye. "And PS, I'm not some young for you to order around, so you can cut that attitude right now."

"You think I'm going to take off on you."

"No, I don't."

"You're lying. And I gave you my word."

You told me you wouldn't hurt me, she thought. *Not the same.*

"I need you," she said. "That's my reality. You want to talk about trust? Then tell me where we're going—"

Abruptly, they both looked up the mountain flank at the same time. The scents of three males were obvious in the descending breeze.

The prisoner took her arm in a hard grip and pulled her behind a hemlock tree. "You get your ass back in there and let me take care of this."

"No." She glared at him. "I'm a helluva shot. You need me even if your ego says you don't—and spare me the he-man bullcrap."

Tension crackled between them, made worse because there were so many things unsaid.

"I'm *not* arguing with you," he said.

"Good, the less we talk, the better."

He clearly meant it in the other way, as in there was no discussion because he was right and that was that. But surprise! Free will applied to females, too—

"Hold on," she said as she refocused on the trees ahead. "They're shifting their positions."

Duran got quiet, narrowing his eyes even

though his nose, like hers, was what was doing the work.

Sure enough, the scents were coming at a different angle now and not because she and Duran had jumped behind the hemlock.

"You said Chalen tried to get the location of his beloved from you." She kept her voice down. "So assuming they're his guards, they're just tracking us. They're not going to kill us—at least not until we lead them where Chalen wants to go himself."

Fury darkened Duran's stare. "There's an easy solution to this."

He took off at a dead run without any warning, his powerful body bursting out from behind the tree so fast, there was no way she could have grabbed onto him—not that she was strong enough to hold him back anyway.

With a curse, Ahmare dematerialized and triangulated a short ascent that put her directly behind, and upwind of, the trio of males. Sure enough, they were dressed in Chalen's uniform, and taking cover behind a group of boulders. No weapons out, but there were knives all over them.

The second she resumed form, her scent registered to them, and the guards wheeled around.

"I can't have you with us, boys." She shook her

head as she pointed her gun at them. "Please don't make me have to take care of this problem—"

The crashing and crunching sounds of something huge barreling through the forest got loud and grew louder, Duran's approach like a tank crushing all that was in its path.

She spoke faster. "I'm going to ask you to leave. If I find you anywhere near us again, I will take it as an attack even if there are no weapons in your hands. Do you understand me?"

They didn't have time to respond. Duran arrived with a roar, and as he went for the guard on the right, Chalen's males palmed daggers.

Their former prisoner was too fast for them.

Duran picked up the first guard he came to and spun around, going discus on the male, slinging him into a tree. As a terrible crack sounded out— like the trunk split from the impact—he smiled like pure evil at the other two, fangs descending.

"I know you," he growled. "Both of you."

His attack on those who had hurt him was vengeance in motion, payback for suffering he had endured, and it was bloody and ugly, limbs bitten clean through, bones broken, heads split on knee and by elbow. The damage was one-sided. All one-sided.

Ahmare shrank back from the fight, especially as Duran killed one by twisting the head so far around that bloodshot, bolt-wide eyes stared out over the guard's own shoulders. It was too close to Rollie. But there was no looking away or leaving, even as the second guard tried to drag himself out of range, his hands clawing at the fallen pine needles and the loose, muddy earth to put distance between him and his previous prisoner.

The male didn't have a chance.

As Duran shoved the loose, dead body of the guard with the over-the-shoulder stare aside, he roared, the animal Ahmare had first witnessed in that cell not only out of its cage, but free of any restraints of decency that civilized vampires held.

There was no stopping him—but she didn't even think to, and not because she was afraid of being collateral damage. His violence made her think about that trigger box and how he'd had to use it to orgasm. How he'd strained and concentrated and tried to find that which should have been a natural and beautiful consequence of making love . . . and in the end, had needed pain to find his release.

It was because of what these males had done to him.

Are you okay?

Yes, are you?

And now, *I know you. Both of you.*

Healer she may have been, but she didn't feel the need to save people from the consequences of being evil and doing wrong. And this was so personal, so visceral, that all of Duran's weapons stayed holstered. This was blood for blood, pain for pain, not a bullet shot from an arm's length away, not a quick-and-it's-over stabbing.

Duran launched himself in the air and pounced on the clawing guard's back. Grabbing a fistful of hair, he yanked back, bared his fangs, and bit into the throat he'd exposed. As he tore flesh away, an arc of arterial blood soared into the air before falling on the ground like paint splashed.

Now Ahmare turned away and put her hands over her mouth. She wasn't sure what she was holding in. Screaming. Crying. Cursing.

So much to choose from.

God, she didn't know how much more she could take.

19

SILENCE.

No, there was breathing, Ahmare realized dimly: Her own, which was high and quick, just the top of her lungs doing the work, and Duran's, which was deep and ragged. She was still wrenched away from him, still with her hands up to her mouth, still . . . with a feeling that she couldn't handle much more.

To get rid of a wave of light-headedness, she forced a long inhale, and that was when the meaty smell of fresh blood and flesh really hit her. Dropping her palms, she knew she had to turn back around so—

Dearest . . . Virgin Scribe.

In the midst of Duran's fang attack, he had flipped the body over, and the carnage was . . . you couldn't even tell what the anatomy had been before his canines had struck. And even now, when there was no more life, at all, in the body of that guard, he was still crouched over his kill like he was waiting for reanimation.

"Duran?" she said.

With a jerk, he looked over at her, his wild eyes unfocused and unblinking, his lower face dripping with blood, his teeth stained red.

"He's gone," Ahmare choked out. "He's not . . . alive anymore."

Duran blinked a number of times. Then looked down at the male underneath him. There was a strangled curse, and Duran fell off to the side, his body landing on his shoulder so that he and the corpse met eyes, one living, one dead, both fixated on the other for two totally different reasons.

Duran put his hands up to his face and rolled onto his back. Then he was twisting again, moving away from the body and onto his hands and knees.

As his head hung, she thought he was going to throw up. He did not.

He reminded her of the way she'd been after Rollie. In shock. Horrified. And it brought her even closer to him. His reaction meant that even though he'd lost it, he hadn't lost himself. Not permanently, anyway. People should be affected by death, especially if they're responsible, no matter the reasons, no matter the justifications.

"Get their weapons," he said hoarsely. "We can always use more."

"Okay."

She was glad for the job. At least until she realized she would have to get near the dead bodies. Steeling herself, she found three daggers, two in the blood-soaked ground, and another on the guard that had had his neck broken. There was no way she was going to pat down the guard that had been savaged. Her stomach was fisting up already—

There was one more to check.

The male who had been thrown against that tree was still alive. Even though he'd hit the trunk like a car that had lost traction on a winter's turn, he was not just breathing, but aware enough that he shrank back against the pine that had nearly paralyzed him.

Beneath a smudge of red hair, his face was

young, and his terrified expression suggested that he'd never seen anything so graphic or violent in his life. His mouth was gaping, little clicking noises coming out as his tongue worked against his teeth, but without a voice box, he could not audibly beg for mercy.

He reminded her of Ahlan: Over his head. Drowning.

About to be killed.

Ahmare approached him with caution, her gun pointed at his chest. "Give me your knife."

As soon as she gave the order, he fumbled with the weapon on his belt, dropping it. Picking it up. Offering it to her hilt down.

"Toss it to my feet," she commanded.

He complied, and she bent over and picked the weapon up, keeping her muzzle on him.

"Any guns?" Duran asked roughly.

In the periphery of her vision, she saw that he was sitting cross-legged now and had wiped his face on his sleeve, his cheeks and chin cleaner, his shirt no different because so much blood had been spilled by him.

"Only knives." She kept her focus on the remaining guard. "One each."

"You're kidding me."

"No." She glanced over. "Why is that a surprise?"

"Toss me one." When she sent the one she'd picked up over at him, there was a pause. "Sonofabitch. They're not working for Chalen."

"What?"

Duran's voice was getting clearer, calmer and closer to normal with every word he spoke. "Chalen keeps careful control over all weapons in his compound. I can remember when they would work on me, it was always an issue about where to find a blade or a gun or a sword on the fly without having to ask the conqueror. They'd get frustrated by this. The only guards who were regularly armed were the ones who monitored the exits and the arsenal." He held up what she'd thrown. "These are handmade shanks. They made them on their off-duty time, probably from cutlery they stole from meals. They are working independently or they'd have better daggers."

"Is this true?" she asked the remaining guard.

The male nodded.

"So you decided to follow us on your own," she prompted. When he shook his head, Duran started to speak, but she talked over him. "You're not the only ones following us." This got a nod. "And you want to stay away from the official trackers because if they find you, you're dead."

"He's dead anyway," Duran said grimly. "I'll see to it myself—"

"Wait," she cut in as Duran got to his feet. "Hold on. Do you recognize this guard?"

Duran came over, his bulk making her feel like she had no control over him—no, actually, that was his mood, not his size, the threat of deadly violence returning to the hard cut of his jaw and the clench of his fists.

"I don't," he said after a moment. "But that doesn't fucking matter—"

"Yes, it does." She refocused on the guard. "Can you stand?"

The young male nodded and got to his feet. It was obvious one of his legs wasn't working right, but other than that, he seemed relatively fine.

"Go," she told him—

"What the fuck!" Duran exploded.

She didn't acknowledge the curse. "Dematerialize now and do not follow us anymore—"

"I'll kill him before—"

Ahmare slapped her palm onto the center of his chest and wadded up the front of his bloodstained shirt. Jerking him down from his towering height, she put herself between him and the guard.

"If he didn't hurt you, let him go."

Duran bared his fangs. "He works for Chalen. You remember, the warlord who is going to kill your fucking brother!"

Ahmare shook her head. "No deaths unless absolutely necessary. In the event I live through this, I'm going to have find peace with what we do for the rest of my nights. And I will not abide killing for the sake of killing. If he didn't hurt you, if he wasn't one of the guards who was in that dungeon with you, you don't get to take his life. That's not revenge. That's evil and no different than Chalen. I will *not* be a part of it."

She kept hold of Duran and pivoted back toward the guard. "Go now. If I see you again, or if he does, I will not stop what comes to you. Do you understand me. This is your warning. I will not step in again and save you."

The young guard nodded. Took a deep breath.

And dematerialized.

As he left, Duran shoved her away and stalked around. When he stopped, it was on the far side of the guard he'd destroyed.

"This is what they're going to do to your brother."

He jabbed his finger at the corpse. "And you just sent a guard back who knows exactly where we are—and may even know where we spent the day if he saw us come out of hiding."

"I have no regrets."

Duran leaned over his kill, hands on hips, chin tilted down so his eyes glowed under his prominent brows. "You will. I promise you, you are going to regret what you just did, and more than likely, your brother is going to pay the price for your misplaced compassion."

Ahmare indicated the carnage with a sweep of her hand. "And you marked our place, too. There's blood all over here and the scent is traveling on the wind. So I suggest that we stop arguing and start moving. If I have to wait through another day, I am going to lose my goddamn fucking mind—"

Duran lurched to one side—caught his balance.

And then passed out, landing with the response-less bounce of a dead body.

20

AHMARE'S FIRST THOUGHT—WELL, SECOND; her first was that Duran had been stabbed somewhere and died from internal blood loss—was not about the cult's location. Chalen. The conqueror's beloved.

It wasn't even about her brother.

Her prevailing thought was, *I don't want to lose this male.*

Duran's life, and its instant of extinction, was the only thing that mattered as she crashed down beside him, her hands going to his chest, her torso bowing over his body as if her back could block the Fade's arrival. His eyes were fixed on the heavens above, staring up to the night sky as if there was a message in it for him, ghostly symbols of the Old Language floating aloft that only he could see.

"Duran?" she breathed as she patted him down.

There was so much blood on his clothes, it was hard to tell what was his and what was from that guard he'd bitten. And a puncture wound of less than an inch could seal itself off on the surface, while the artery underneath became an oil spill in his ocean, ruining everything.

"Duran!" Now she was more urgent. "Are you . . ."

Are you dead?

Dumb-ass question to ask, but that wasn't why she didn't finish the sentence. She feared the answer—

Abruptly, his torso jerked upright with such force and strength, his shoulder punched her, throwing her back. And the inhale he took in was so great, she could have sworn she felt the very draw of it.

"Are you okay?" she said.

Yes, are you?

His head cranked in her direction. His pupils seemed to focus on her properly, and neither was dilated. "Sorry. Don't know what that was."

As she exhaled, she felt like she was doing part two of that inhale of his, finishing the relay, so to speak. "It's all right. But we need to check you out."

He lifted his shirt and they both looked down at the ridges of his abdominals. Nothing. Then he twisted around and offered her an inspection of his spine. There were no wounds there, either.

That took care of the big stuff, she thought. As long as he hadn't been nailed in the groin. Femoral arteries were the superconductors of the lower body, capable of draining blood volume like a tub, but in that case, there would be all kinds of blood seeping through his pants and there was none.

"Let's go," he said as he pushed himself onto his feet.

Ahmare thought he was going to make it to vertical because he was speaking coherently. Nope. He went down again, to a sitting position this time— and given that the plan had been for them to run? Not good.

"I don't know what's wrong with me." He looked at his arms, flipping his hands from palm up to palm down. "Nothing is listening to the commands."

Ahmare scanned the woods, noting that unlike the kudzu-choked forest that buffered the mountain's approach, there was nothing but tree trunks and pine boughs to hide behind here at its base. Considering the lack of ground cover, they were sitting ducks, even though the moon was hazy and that cut down on its glow.

And then there was that anatomy exam of a body, no more than five feet away, a beacon for anyone with a halfway decent nose.

Duran made a second attempt to get up. A third.

As he fell back down that last time, she put two and two together and got an oh-hell as an answer.

"You need to feed," she said roughly.

He recoiled. "No, I'll be okay. I did about two weeks ago."

Frowning, she asked, "Chalen gave you females?"

"It was the only way to keep me alive." He glanced over at the two dead bodies. "And I took those veins just so I could be strong enough for my revenge."

He seemed confused, as if feeding had been part of a bargain with destiny, and he'd kept his side—so why wasn't he strong enough to keep going now?

She let herself go down to her knees and yanked up her sleeve. "Let's do this."

"No." He frowned and pushed her arm away. "No, I'll just—"

"You want to waste time trying to get up a fourth time? I've been counting in case you haven't. And you may have fed fourteen nights ago—" God, she did not want to think of the particulars—and maybe he had been with a female before. Maybe she'd been wrong about that. "—but you know as well as I do that stress and physical exertion will drain the strength fast. And don't try to tell me you didn't just get one hell of a workout because I watched you."

Duran looked off into the woods—as if the idea of her seeing him in that violent state, doing that damage, shamed him.

"Come on," she said, holding her wrist to him again. "This is not a place to get caught, and I don't want to have to drag you back to those boulders. I will if I have to, though."

Ahmare was right.

He did need to feed. Getting away from Chalen, covering the distance, expending the energy he just had . . . it had taken his energy reserve to zero.

And then there was seeing Nexi again.

And Ahmare herself.

All moves on the abacus that had to be balanced by him taking a vein. It was the way biology worked, the setup the Scribe Virgin had created for the species, male taking from female, female taking from male.

"Just do it," she prompted him. Then she rolled her eyes. "God, you've turned me into a Nike commercial."

"What's that?"

"The cult didn't have TV, did it." She brought her wrist to her mouth. "I'm done talking about this."

He almost please-don't-do-that'd her. Because he knew, even before the first scent of her blood hit the air and apparently hopped a ride on a torpedo straight into his nose, that she wasn't going to stop.

And he wasn't going to be able to say no.

Duran wasn't even clear why denying himself her vein was so critical. He and Nexi had fed each other when they needed to, and they hadn't even had sex. It had just been a no-big-deal exchange of the necessary, one for the other—well, at least on his side, it had been that way. And it should be that way with Ahmare, too—

Not. Even. Close.

As she scored herself and put her wrist directly onto his lips, it became immediately clear that "no big deal" was not at all applicable to Ahmare.

"Everything in the Whole Fucking World" might have covered it.

No, that didn't go far enough. How about "Universe."

Everything in the Whole Fucking Universe and an Infinity Past That.

Dearest Virgin Scribe, that barely described the first draw of her precious blood, the first welling inside his mouth . . . the first swallow down his throat. His body, once his own, became hers to control, an extension of her will and direction sure as if he were just another of her limbs, dictated by her and her alone, no part of him his own at this moment.

And forevermore, he suspected.

Which had been the true why of his "no." On some level, probably the one closest to his survival skills, he had known that there was no going back now. The taste of her, the vitality that blasted through every cell in his body, the tingling, springing, full-tilt-and-then-some that flooded him was at once blinding and telescopically clarifying—

Moaning.

Something was moaning—it was him. Sounds were rising up his throat, and getting no further than that because he was too busy gulping down the wine, the beautiful wine, the astounding, incredible, transforming wine of her blood.

He fell back—either that or the earth came up to support him. And as a bed of soft, fragrant pine needles caught and held him, nature's mattress, Ahmare accommodated the shift, moving closer, keeping the connection as he continued to drink.

Unlike him, she was not focused on the feeding.

She had oriented herself with her back to the mountain's ascent, no doubt so that she could catch with her nose any scents carried down on the drafts from the summit. She had a gun in her free hand, and she was sweeping the muzzle in a slow panorama of what was to the left, right, and center of them. As the barrel moved, so, too, did her head, but the two went in opposite directions.

So that either her gun's sight, or her eyesight, covered or could cover them.

In her watchful protection of him during this most vulnerable time, he knew to his core that she would get deadly if she had to defend him—and she would succeed. She was fierce, but not agitated. Alert, but not afraid. Aggressive, but only if she had to be.

Tears pricked at the corners of his eyes, and not just because someone was protecting him. It was because he hated that she was in a situation where such defenses needed to be put up. God, he wished he could have brought something to her life other than his body's need . . . just after she'd been forced to watch his revenge manifest itself all over two other living things.

Even if those guards had been ones who had enjoyed hurting him.

"Keep taking," she told him without looking down. "I only want to stop once for this."

Duran closed his eyes and felt a stab in his heart. In the midst of his ecstatic spell, he would do well to keep in mind that this was not a beginning for them. A launching pad to grow closer. A foundation on which to build.

This was biology in wartime.

And when the hell had he gotten to be such a romantic, anyway?

21

AHMARE HAD TO GIVE him credit.

Duran took only what he needed, and then he lapped the wound closed with his tongue and got right to his feet. Usually after a feeding, there was a lull of laziness, a post-vein glow that floated anyone who had just been nourished in a placid pool of satiation. But he was clearly ignoring all that in favor of what she needed from him.

He required blood. She required movement.

So after he nodded to her—a thank-you, she

guessed—he pointed to the west and started to run, going slowly at first, and then with increasing speed. Soon enough, the two of them were making an expert marathoner's time through the forest.

With the wind in her face, and her body on exertion autopilot, her senses were alive, ready to find in the woodland landscape pursuers, aggressors, trackers . . . murderers. She searched what was to the sides of them, and to the rear, her eyes pulling shadows out from behind trees and large boulders, isolating trunks as possible covers, identifying hideouts in fallen logs and stumps.

Duran was doing the same, and the focus they needed on their environment was a good reminder of the reason they were together, of the purpose of this intersection of their lives. The forced intimacy of those daylight hours, which had led to some very naked skin on very naked skin, was exactly like that feeding just now.

A side step, not the ultimate goal.

And in a way, she was grateful. Otherwise, her brain, riding a high of chemicals cooked up by his mouth on her wrist, might have carried her off into an oblivion she could not afford to visit, much less live in—

"Over there," he said. "That's the entry."

Those were the first words he'd spoken since they'd started running, and the fact that they were no more breathless than if he'd had his feet up on a sofa and a sleeping cat on his chest made her stupidly proud. But come on, like she had any control over the contents of her blood or how it nourished him?

Still, she felt as though she mattered, and not just in some ephemeral emotional sense, but in a nuts-and-bolts, chassis, gas-tank kind of way.

It seemed more reliable, more tangible, than what had happened between them in the bunker.

As they came up to an old hunting shack, a nothing-special relic that seemed more likely to have been built and abandoned centuries ago by humans hunting for food instead of sport, unease went through her—and it was a surprise to realize the anxiety didn't have anything to do with the fact that they were about to break into a cult.

Duran was going to have to go back to Chalen, wasn't he.

That had been the plan that she'd made with the conqueror. She had agreed that she would take the weapon he gave her, use it to get his female . . . and return it to him. If she didn't, Ahlan wasn't getting out of that castle alive.

"It doesn't look like much," Duran said as he opened a door that was more air hole than board and nail. When she didn't immediately follow, he looked over his shoulder. "What?"

His return to that cell had been slightly less traumatic when she hadn't cared about him. When she'd thought of him as "the prisoner." Now, she knew she was going to lose one or the other: If she let Duran go free, her brother was dead, and blood-line always should win, right?

"Sorry," she mumbled as she forced herself through the flimsy door.

Inside, the cabin was barren and rotting, noth-ing but dust and pine tree debris, the forest reclaim-ing the construction. The passage of time had made that which should have been durable just another biodegradable carcass, a bag of bones soon to be-come dirt save for the pick-up sticks of nails and the two four-paned windows that would survive longer.

"Over here," he said as he went across to the far corner.

As his heavy weight made the floorboards groan, she hoped for his sake there was no lower level. He was liable to fall through.

Crouching down, he tucked his fingertips into a

knot in a board, and as he lifted, he brought up a three-by-five section that was more solid than you'd think.

"We go down here."

Ahmare went over and didn't accept the hand he put out to help her descend a ladder that was just thin cross-hatches tied to two poles with twine. As she carefully lowered herself, her sinuses became filled with a complex bouquet of rot and mold and mud, and she decided, if she got out of this alive, she was going to Disney World.

Okay, fine. Not Disney World, because really, how was a vampire going to handle the land of sunshine, sunscreen, and screeching human children. But she was going to go somewhere where they had air-conditioning and air fresheners and beds with clean sheets. Running water. A refrigerator.

A shower with multiple heads.

Or how about just warm water.

With both her brother and Duran.

Ahmare got to the ground and flicked the light of her phone on. Plastered walls, the earth held back by what looked like clay packing. Dirt floor. And ahead, a narrow passageway, the terminal of which her illumination could not reach.

Duran jumped down, as if he knew that his bulk

was going to make kindling out of that ladder. "We go that way."

Not that there was another option.

"Wait," she said. "You need to close the hatch."

"No." He flicked on his flashlight and pointed it into the void, the beam perfectly round and distinct as it widened from the pinpoint of the bulb, like something out of a Nancy Drew illustration. "At this stage of the game, I want Chalen's guards to follow us."

As he started off, striding fast, she followed. "Are you crazy?"

"Trust me."

Duran's skin was alive with warning as he strode through the damp and cold passageway. It wasn't because anyone was behind them.

On the contrary, it was what lay ahead.

He knew the turns and the straightaways by heart. Knew also that this stretch of their entry was the most dangerous. In all other parts of this infiltration, they had options, defensible covers, vistas to bolt off into. Here? If for some reason their presence had been sensed and the *Dhavos*'s defenders were sent out, they would have to rely on a direct, hand-to-hand fight. And with him still logy from the feeding?

He doubted either one of them would survive.

And feared the even worse outcome of his father taking Ahmare prisoner.

On top of that, there was the risk represented by Chalen's guards, but he needed them. The cult would currently be centralized at the arena doing the nightly "ablution" ceremony whereby they were washed in a metaphysical sense of their sins of the previous twenty-four hours by the *Dhavos*. Assuming that practice hadn't changed, this was going to give him and Ahmare a chance to get in, get disguised, and get going. Chalen's guards, on the other hand, weren't going to be as efficient as he and Ahmare in finding their way around—and when they were discovered, chaos was going to ensue.

A perfect smoke screen for him and Ahmare to hide inside as they got the beloved. And then he pared off and did what he had come to do.

A final curve in the passageway and they were at the vault door. This one was similar to the one he had put on the bunker and, in fact, had been his inspiration.

Stopping, he went for the keypad, and entered the six-digit code that he'd gotten from spying on a defender using it inside the compound.

No backup plan. If this didn't—

"Is it working?" Ahmare said.

"It's the right code." He reentered the digits. "At least it used to be."

As he waited, his heart pounded in his—

"The pound key!" he said as he hit the symbol.

With a clunk and a grind, there was a shift of gears, and then . . . they were in.

The air that escaped was dry and many degrees warmer than the draft-and-damp they were in. But the smell of it, the over-conditioned, not-even-close-to-natural, piped-through-tinny-ducts sting in his sinuses rode ingrained neuropathways to the oldest part of his brain.

The part that had been forged when he'd been young and his *mahmen* had still been alive—and life had been all about her suffering.

"Are you going to go inside?"

Ahmare asked the question quietly, as if she knew he was locked in place. And the truth was, 99 percent of him was screaming for him to pull a turn-around-now and sprint back to that rickety ladder. In his instant fantasy, he was free to escape through the forest, backtrack to the ATV, and take off with Ahmare, running from Chalen and from his father, free to be in a world with only the two of them.

It was a nice piece of fiction.

In reality, he had Chalen's tracking collar around his neck, a conscience that would not let his *mahmen*'s death go, and her brother stuck in a hell Duran himself had been in for two decades.

"Yes," he said roughly. "I'm going in."

Crossing the threshold made him ill, and he paused again. But then he looked back at Ahmare. She, too, was hesitating, in the way you'd pause if you had a gun in your hand that might, or might not, blow up in your face if you pulled its trigger. And that wasn't about where they were going. It was clearly about her guide.

He reached out a hand. "I know where we have to go. I'm not going to let you down."

As she focused over his shoulder, he was well aware of what she saw: darkness, thick in a way only the subterranean shadow could be.

She did not take his palm, just as she hadn't taken it as he'd wanted to help her down the ladder. It was as if she had to prove to herself she could go it alone, even if that was not how she was proceeding in—and he could respect that.

But he needed her to hear something.

He put his hand on her shoulder, and she must have read something in his face because she went still. "Listen to me," he said. "There are four exits in the compound, one at each point of north, south, east, and west. This is the easterly one. They all dump out in various ways at the base of the mountain. The codes are six digits, and they progress, starting with the northern one."

He ran through the sequences with her and she got them quick, repeating them to him. "And the pound sign," he added. "Don't forget the pound at the end. If anything happens to me or we get separated, you need to find one of the spokes in the wheel. The compound is set up in a centralized plan around the intersection of the four compass points. The corridors that curve are not what you want because they'll just keep you in a circle. The straight ones take you either out to the exits or down to the arena, you got it? Those are what will save you, and you'll know you're heading out instead of in because everyone else will be going in the opposite direction, in case the alarm is sounded."

"Okay. Right."

"One more thing. This whole mountain is

rigged with explosives. You will have three minutes once the red lights come on." Duran didn't bother to keep the bitterness out of his voice. "The congregation is brainwashed by the *Dhavos*. They believe once those red lights start flashing, the end of the universe has arrived and they are supposed to be praying. Do not try to save anyone. Let them go to the arena, they've made their decision because of their delusions and that's their destiny. Nexi and I are the only two people I know who've broken out of it. You are not going to win that debate, and more to the point, you need to get yourself out, okay? Do *not* try to save anyone. You're the only one who matters."

She nodded. And then, "Duran . . . thank you. For everything."

He stared at her face. There was a dirt smudge at her temple, fine curls had escaped her ponytail, and the flush of their exertion to get to the cabin had dulled in the cool temperature of the underground passageway.

Her eyes met his like she was reading his mind.

As they both went in for the kiss, he knew this was good-bye. One, or both of them, was not making it out of this suicide mission alive.

And what worried him most was that she

maybe didn't get his message. When he told her not to save anyone . . . it included himself.

Chances were good she was going to have to leave him behind when the mountain blew, and he prayed her need to save her brother's life was going to override the light that glowed, soft, warm, and kind, in her eyes as she stared up at him now.

"No one matters but you," he said roughly.

22

As Duran spoke, Ahmare did not like the expression on his face. Nope. Not at all.

"Don't forget me, okay?" he said softly. "You don't have to mourn me, but just . . . I want someone to remember me."

"I'm not hearing this—"

"Just in case the Fade is a lie, I don't want it to be like I never existed at all."

Before she could argue with him, he squeezed her hand and then reached around and pulled the vault almost shut. Without another word, he started off, and it was as Ahmare stared after him in despair that she noticed a glow far off in the dark distance.

It wasn't a security light. Running to catch up with him, the illumination was seeping around the jambs of a closed door.

There was no keypad this time. Just a garden-variety handle like the ones in her gym, and given what waited for them on the other side, she felt like the portal should have come with surgeon general's warnings, an airbag, and a crash helmet.

"One . . . two . . ." Duran gripped the handle. "Three."

He didn't slam the release down; he lowered it and pulled the door open. Leaning out, he kept his gun by his side.

"To the left. Fast and quiet."

They slipped out into a pale gray corridor that had all the nuance and distinction of what she imagined the cult members to have: everything buffed to a low polish, no ornamentation, the ceiling, walls, and floor covered by late-sixties-era linoleum squares, the seams of which were showing fine lines of glue that had discolored into a mustard-yellow seepage. Fluorescent lights were set in bald panels every six feet along the ceiling, and many of the tubes were blinking or burned out. Underfoot, the tiles had been worn in two distinct lanes running parallel to each other.

From people walking in lines or in pairs.

The sense she had of entering a foreign world was reinforced as they came upon a door with a handle just the same as the first. A fake wood placard had been stuck on the panel at eyeball height, the white letters etched into the plastic reading, "Modesty Comes First."

Off in the distance, there was an odd, disquieting hum.

Duran looked around with a frown. Then he shook his head.

"Let me go in first," he said as he curled his hand onto the lever.

She glanced behind them. No one was in the corridor. Nor were there people moving around, at least not that she could hear or sense, and she wondered just how huge the facility was.

Duran moved in quick silence, opening the door and disappearing into an interior that, going by the sign, gave Ahmare images of old Kotex pad ads, and bathing suits that had skirts and built-in bras, and pantyhose that were more like compression stockings.

Maybe this was where the human race sent their maiden aunts when they couldn't stand the whisker-chinned, lipstick-smudged kisses for one more holiday season—

What the *hell* was that hum?

Duran popped his head out. "There's something wrong here."

"You think?" she muttered to herself.

He pulled her inside, and she gasped, nearly jumping back out into the corridor. The vast room, which had to be forty feet long and twenty feet wide, was swarming with flies—no, not flies, moths. A thousand pale-winged moths were in the air, fluttering in disjointed flight paths, knocking into each other, billiard balls without the felt and the pockets.

Batting them away from her face, the smell was horrible, like the sludge of a late August riverbed, stagnant, wet, rotting.

She flapped her hand around again, even though it was useless. There were too many—

"Is this the laundry?" she said.

"Used to be."

There were industrial washers and tumble dryers on one side. On the other, racks and racks . . . an entire department store of racks . . . on which hundreds of maroon wool robes hung in various stages of decay. The moths were living off the fabric, chewing holes that were ever expanding, leaving bolts of shredded material in their wake.

It was an entire ecosystem, the result of two moths, or three, being imported into the environment, whereupon housekeeping had been set up and the Mr. and Mrs. had Left It to Beaver like a trillion times.

Duran went over and pulled a robe free. The wool powdered in his hands, falling onto his boots, autumn leaves without the season or the tree, just the molting.

"Unwearable." He dropped the shawl collar. "I'd assumed we'd be able to camouflage ourselves and thus integrate into the congregation."

Ahmare felt the hand of death tickle the back of her neck. "Do you think we're going to need to?"

As Duran went back out into the corridor and held the door open for Ahmare, moths escaped like a puff of smoke from a burning room, flitting out in a scatter. He almost felt like shooing them back in so they weren't left out of the party.

On his nod, he and Ahmare doubled back the way they'd come, proceeding along one side of the curving corridor, crouched but moving at a steady pace with guns up. As they passed by the entry where they'd come in and ran into nobody coming to check why the door had not been fully closed . . . as they approached the cafeteria's kitchen and there were no lingering smells of food being cooked or having been eaten . . . as silence and stuffy air were the only accompaniment to their infiltration . . . a terrible conclusion began to form in his mind.

And he fought it.

Fought it like he should have been battling the *Dhavos*'s defenders.

When they came up to the intersection of the next spoke, the one that ran north-south, he leaned out and looked around. No one. No one talking. Walking. And not just because of the ablution ceremony.

"This way," he said.

As he spoke, he could hear the rage in his own voice, and his body started to tremble with aggression.

Overhead, fluorescent lights flickered, more of

them out as they zeroed in on the arena, the illumination a herky-jerk that juiced up the warnings already screaming in his head.

Memories came back to him, things he wished he could unsee. His mother's eyes, wide in a bruised face, brimming with tears she was trying to hold in. Her quiet, desperate courage to put one foot in front of the other because she was terrified her son would be taken away by her abuser. The years of suffering that she had borne.

Because of Duran.

You are my reason for living, my blessing, she'd always told him.

Bullshit, he was her curse. And killing his sire had struck him as the only thing he could do to earn the love he had never deserved from her.

The only way he could live with himself.

As he closed in on the arena, he felt chased even though he repeatedly looked behind himself and almost wanted to see hordes of armed defenders bearing down on his neck. But . . . no. No matter how many times he glanced over his shoulder or checked out an intersection of a curving corridor, there was nobody around them.

No alarms going off.

Just the pair of worn paths in the linoleum un-

derfoot and the fluorescent tubes spasming overhead.

"My *mahmen* died the night before I was ab-
ducted."

As Ahmare's head jerked toward him, he realized that he'd spoken the words aloud.

"I am so sorry—"

He interrupted her. "She died, I believe, of a
heart attack. She and I were in our cell, and she had
been tired for a number of nights. And with that off
stomach. Suddenly, she just . . ." He shook his head.
"She was sitting on her pallet and she put her hand
under her arm, like she had a sudden pain. Then
she was holding the front of her chest and gasping
for air. She looked at me."

"Oh, Duran."

It was helpful that they were rushing down the
spoke, focused on any attacks, busy, busy, busy. He
doubted he would have been able to get through
the story otherwise.

"She slumped over to the side. She was still staring at me, but I don't think she could see me anymore. I started yelling her name. I sat her up, but
her head . . . it was lolling to her shoulder, then it
fell . . . back."

He was unaware of having slowed to a stop. But

one of the four sets of double doors into the arena was in front of them.

"One of the defenders—the *Dhavos*'s private guard—came in because he heard me yelling. The *Dhavos* then ran into our room. I went for his throat. I just fucking . . ." He closed his eyes. "It took seven defenders to get me off him, and as soon as he was free, he fell all over himself to get to her body. She was going gray by then, the color leaving her. He cried. All over her. They had to drag me out of that room. They stuck me with something, a needle. I blacked out."

He stared at the closed double doors. The wooden panels had been carved with the profile of a male whose features were identical to his own.

Duran looked in the direction they'd come one last time. "She arrived here as a lost soul, and she bought into the lies, into the greatness, into the saving. And then he ruined her in all the ways that mattered. He did that to a lot of people, but she was the one who mattered to me." He cleared his throat. "The next night, after they'd drugged me, I woke up back in the room alone. Her body was gone. Her pallet. It was as if he had erased her. I decided I would honor her memory, do her Fade ceremony anyway. He wasn't going to take that away from her. I went to the bathroom. I showered and I shaved so that I would be clean. It didn't matter that I had no remains. I told myself it would still work. I would say the words, make the movements, do the ritual even if I had to pantomime it. If the Scribe Virgin was truly the benevolent mother of the race, I told myself, she would grant my *mahmen* dispensation."

"I'm sure your *mahmen* is in the Fade—"

"You don't know that. Neither do I." He rubbed his eyes. "They hit me over the head and I came to in Chalen's great hall in front of his hearth. On his table. My father was smart. He knew what I was going to do as soon as the Fade ceremony was done. I was going to have two dead parents before midnight, and nothing was going to stop me."

Duran put his hand on the right side of the door. On the profile of his father's face. "I was so close to getting her out, too. It was a fulcrum of events coming together. The bunker was ready, our escape route planned, my supplies set at Nexi's. I had helped Nexi get out of the compound as a test the week before, and it had worked. I'd needed to make sure it would work, you see . . . I had to be certain my *mahmen* would be safe."

When Ahmare put her hand on his shoulder, he

jumped and focused on her. In a low voice, he said, "I was so close. I was *so* fucking close."

As he spoke, he wasn't sure whether he was talking about getting his mother free.

Or what he had come to do here on this night.

Duran pushed the door and stepped into the arena.

23

THE SKELETONS WERE EVERYWHERE. Hundreds of them, maybe more.

As Ahmare followed Duran into a theater area that had rows upon rows of seats descending to a central stage, she couldn't count the bones.

And they had died horribly. These people . . . these poor people had suffered.

She lowered her gun and went over to the topmost section of seats. "Dear . . . God."

Duran walked down the carpeted stairs that were covered with brown stains. Blood, she realized. They must have bled out, but from what?

Duran bent down and picked up a syringe. "Hemlock."

Her brain struggled to process it all. "I saw those trees in the woods?"

"My father grew them for this purpose." Duran put the syringe back precisely where he had found it. "Deadly to humans. Worse to vampires if injected. You bleed out of every orifice."

Which explained that thick brown staining, which had dried . . . some time ago . . . into the runners on the stairs, and in the aisles, and all over the seats and backs of the chairs.

She could only imagine the carnage when it had first happened.

"He always said he would do it." Duran walked downward to the stage, stepping over arms and legs. Rib cages. Skulls. "He talked about end of days, and I always thought he must have gotten the idea from the human media or something because we don't go by the term 'days.' And you were right, TV and newspapers and radios were all barred to us, but he kept track of the outside world with them. Sometimes he would bring clippings in to my *mahmen* and read them to her, especially before I went through my transition."

"How old are you?" Ahmare blurted.

"A year out of the change." He shook his head. "I mean, I was a year out of it when she died and I ended up at Chalen's. Nexi was the one who helped me through my transition, and I in turn helped her get out."

Duran bent over and gingerly moved an arm bone back into place. "He told them every night at sunset they were with sin. He told them he was the salvation. They believed him. This"—he motioned around the arena—"was supposed to be the cleansing. I imagine when they first injected themselves they were in a flush of obedience, so sure they were doing the right thing and this would take them to the next level of consciousness with their leader. They didn't want to go to the Fade. It was a mental and emotional elevation they were seeking and that he promised to deliver."

He picked up a thigh bone and looked at the length. "But then the pain set in. I saw him inject a male once. He did it in front of me as a threat. The male was so prepared for it, offering his vein readily, no one restraining him. My father made the male kneel before him, and he kissed the male on the forehead, cupping his face, smiling down at him with warmth and compassion. Then he told the male to close his eyes and accept the gift."

Duran replaced the femur and walked farther down. When he got to the bottom of the seating bowl, he went around and mounted five steps up onto the dais. "My father looked at me as he injected the cult member, and then he embraced the male, as if all I had to do was submit to the rules and all my problems would go away. Except"—he laughed harshly—"the asshole would of course still be beating and abusing my *mahmen*. I watched as the male leaned into my father. The male was smiling—until he wasn't. His eyes popped open. The whites of them turned red. And then the blood came. Out of his mouth as he coughed. Out of his nose. Out of his ears as he fell to the side. His breathing turned into gurgles, and he contorted, first stretching back on his spine, then curling in tight. He bled . . . from everywhere.

"And the most fucked-up thing?" Duran looked up at her. "My father stepped back and seemed shocked by it all. Like what the fuck did he think was going to happen? Did he actually believe his own bullshit about transcendence? I never thought he did, but maybe he expected a bolt of light to come through the ceiling and bathe that male in enlightenment." There was a pause. "That's when I knew he was going to have to get rid of me. Even without the issue of my *mahmen*, I had witnessed his confusion and knew that he was just making it all up. I saw behind the curtain that night, and in a world built on the illusion of his superiority, that could not abide."

Ahmare started down the stairs, imagining all of the suffering. The people had been sitting in the chairs at first, but that hadn't lasted. The bones were in the aisles, in the spaces between the seats, on the steps. It was difficult to tell for sure which ribs went with what arms or whether a skull was with the right spine as the bodies had intertwined, perhaps seeking comfort from each other as they realized, too late, that the promise was not coming. Only the pain.

"So this was his doomsday," Duran said. "But he wouldn't have stuck around. I knew he had an evac plan because he told my *mahmen* and she told me. He never planned to die with his flock, and he was going to take her with him. He used to say, 'If the red lights start to flash, we have three minutes before the compound blows apart. I will come and get you.' I guess the explosives failed."

As Ahmare got to the bottom, she wanted to throw up. The blood had rivered down the aisles and pooled around the base of the stage, called by gravity toward the focal point, the last offering to an evil, mortal god.

Her boots left prints, as if she were walking on the silt of a dried riverbed—and she thought of Rollie's missing head, and his blood on the dirt, spreading out like the Mississippi River. It had glistened in the night. Was it dry now? Yes, and some of it would have been absorbed into the thirsty earth.

She looked over at Duran and didn't know what to say. It was all too much.

His eyes swung back to her. "I never knew his name."

"I'm sorry?"

"The male who died in front of me. I never knew anyone's name—well, except for Nexi, and she told it to me only after I got her to the bunker, when she was thanking me. I informed her it was a team effort, and that was the truth. She was the one who figured out the escape route and the timing of it all. She's brilliant like that."

He looked around again. "You know, my *mahmen* used to tell me her father's name all the time. I couldn't figure out why, but now . . . I think she wanted to give it to me. She couldn't quite get there, though."

Ahmare knew that she would never forget what he looked like, the risen son, his hair chopped by a blade's thin edge, his eyes wary and pained, his big body magnificent and unbowed under all he had endured.

And there was that collar around his throat, locked on tight, blinking a red light.

It was a symbol of everything that had marked his life: He had never been free. He had been ever a captive.

"What was her father's name?" Ahmare said hoarsely.

"It doesn't matter now." He paused. "Theo. It was . . . Theo."

Going around, she ascended the five steps and joined him on the stage. The view from the focal point of the arena was gruesome, the full magnitude of the deaths the stuff of nightmares.

How could anyone do this to other people? she wondered. It was murder even though the cult members had volunteered for it.

"We'll see about the beloved now," Duran said. "Enough of the past."

Lost in his story, she had forgotten about everything else—except . . . "Oh, God, was your *mahmen* Chalen's female, too?"

He laughed in a short, hard burst. "No."

"But then she'll be dead, too, right? The *Dhavos* must have killed Chalen's female, too. Or . . . did he leave and take her with them?"

Shit, her brother.

"We'll find out. This way—"

"Wait." She stopped him. "First this."

He turned around with expectation on his face, like he was ready to answer a question. That expression changed quick as she took the trigger to his collar out of her holster.

Placing the black box on the floor between them, she lifted her boot over the control. "You deserve your freedom. Just the same as everyone else."

With that, she slammed her steel-reinforced sole down with all the anger she felt at what had been done to him, to his *mahmen*, to all the innocent, wayward souls who had died here.

The trigger box broke into pieces. The red light on the front of the collar dimmed.

And was extinguished.

It was an incomplete freedom, of course, as he would never not be tied to the circumstances of his birth or the terrible acts of his father. But he could choose his path forward. Just as she had chosen a path forward from the deaths of her parents.

No one else at the helm.

"What have you done?" he whispered.

"Fuck Chalen," she replied.

24

W HAT ABOUT YOUR BROTHER?"
As Duran asked the question, he
knew Ahmare had already answered it
by crushing the trigger to his restraint collar. But he
wanted to make sure he understood what she
meant.

"I'll save you both." She shook her head. "That's
the way this has to end. I cannot accept any other
outcome."

He glanced out at the skeletons and then

thought of the empty corridors of the facility. It seemed cruel to mention that outcomes were not always acceptable. That sometimes they were even worse than *un*-acceptable. But he appreciated what she was doing for him, what it implied . . . what it meant.

An impulse to kiss her mouth occurred to him, but not here. Not in the space where all these deaths had occurred—it would be like turning something special into a bad omen, as if the setting could contaminate the contact.

"Thank you," he said in a voice that cracked.

She grasped one of his hands and squeezed. Her eyes were wide with emotion. "Let's do what we need to and get out of here."

Duran nodded and led them off stage to the right, to the back of the house where the lighting and AV equipment were dust-covered and long asleep. He imagined, as they weeded in and out of the various theater lamps and speakers, that all of the equipment was antiquated now. Twenty years down the line and there would have been improvements, right? As with Ahmare's car, the styling and buttons and screens of which he had not recognized or understood, there would be new technology, advancement, refinements.

That was not going to be the case for him, however.

He knew, on the same deep level that had gotten him through Chalen's dungeon, that he was not going to progress past all this. There would be no technological improvement to him, no advancement . . . no refinement.

Collar or not, freedom or not, he would be ever among the skeletons here in his father's arena, his mortal animation an insufficient distinguishing characteristic from the *Dhavos*'s dead. Made sense. Though he moved, his soul, his vital animation, had died out long ago.

In this respect, whether he made it out of here alive or not wasn't going to matter.

"The trapdoor is here," he said as he beckoned Ahmare down a cramped staircase.

At the bottom, the door was locked, but he entered the correct code and the pound key, and there was that shift inside the panels and the wall.

Pushing the way open, he flicked on his flashlight. The beam pierced the darkness and reflected gold. Gleaming, resonant gold.

"Oh, my God," Ahmare breathed.

"A suitable entry hall for a god, right?" Duran muttered.

"Is it real?" she said as they started down the passageway.

"I think so." He put his hand out and found the wall cool and smooth to the touch. "They were required to give him all their worldly assets if they joined. Houses, cars, jewelry, clothes. There are sorting rooms in the compound, everything segregated and valued for resale."

"To think eBay didn't exist back then."

"What's eBay?" Then he glanced over his shoulder. "I was the only young at the compound. He made them give away their offspring as well, telling them that sacrifice was necessary and paramount, but I think that was, like everything else he said, just bullshit. What he was really worried about was that their concern over the welfare of their young might at some point supersede their devotion to him. Unacceptable."

No matter how quietly he put his boots down, the sound of his footfalls reverberated in the gold colon that dumped out at his father's private quarters. Old habits of being silent died hard, and he became uncomfortable with the sound.

"I was strong even as a pretrans," he told her. "And I found duct work in our bedroom cell that

allowed me to travel through the ceilings and ob-
serve the cult's layout and schedule of meditations
and supplications. When I found the laundry room
and the robes, I could even walk around during the
night, blending in. Watching from under the hood.
I got good at stealing things." He looked up at the
gold-leafed ceiling. "I'll bet if you go into the ducts
even now my stashes of clothes, car keys, glasses,
and shoes were where I left them. I was a hoarder,
and it was all about outfitting myself and my
mahmen for when we got out."

"How many people died back there?"

"Depends on when he ordered them dead.
There were over three hundred people in the cult
when I was taken out of here. Maybe it continued
to grow, I don't know. Maybe it faded. It depends on
when he played the end of days card. He certainly
intended to add to his flock. There was an expan-
sion of this facility"—he tapped the wall—"about
two years before I left. That was how I found the
human contractors to build the bunker, and I paid
them with money I took out of his vault."

"He let humans down here?"

"What choice did he have? If he'd used members
of our species and it had gotten back to Wrath or

the Council? He had to use humans and he paid them well enough to ask no questions, work at night, and keep their eyes to themselves."

They came up to a solid gold door. As he entered the passcode and pound key, he swallowed through a tight throat.

And then . . . .

After the lock released, he opened the panel wide and pointed his flashlight into the darkness.

"Holy . . . shit," Ahmare whispered.

<hr>

It was Creed Bratton from *The Office*, Ahmare thought as she walked into a sumptuously appointed bedroom. Clicking on her own cell phone's light, she shone her beam around.

The unimaginable luxury made her remember the clip of Creed looking into the camera and saying, "I've been involved in a number of cults. You have more fun as a follower. But you make more money as a leader."

Given the way those poor souls had died back in the arena, the former was obviously not true, and she hated that her brain coughed up something so pop-culture'y because it seemed disrespectful to those who had lost their lives. But as she looked at the pastel silk walls, and the draped silk bunting over the circular bed, and the satin sheets bearing the profile that had been etched on those double doors at the arena, she decided the "more money as a leader" thing was clearly right in this case.

No linoleum here. The carpet was thick and fine-napped and—

"The murals," she said as she swung her light around.

An enormous scene of a garden, with a fountain in the center and birds in midflight and beds filled with flowers, graced the smooth plaster, obviously painted by somebody who knew what they were doing. And as if it was not an artist's rendering but rather a picture window, or perhaps an open arch to the great outdoors, drapes had been mounted around the artwork, the swoops of sunshine-yellow damask held back so the "view" wasn't blocked.

A representation of Utopia, a beautiful, impossible-for-a-vampire, daylight-not-reality that nonetheless captivated.

It was rather like the bill of false goods the *Dhavos* had sold his congregation.

"You want Chalen's beloved," Duran said. "Here it is."

She pivoted around, lowering her light so she

didn't nail him in the eye. Duran was over by the bed, standing next to a shadow box that had been installed into the wall.

As Ahmare approached, she focused on what he was illuminating. Something was set back behind the glass . . . something that glowed.

"A pearl?" she breathed. Then she remembered the conqueror's decrepit body on his throne. "Of course. Chalen's crown had an empty mounting in front—and that is what went in it."

"The *Dhavos* wasn't just a spiritual leader, he was a good businessman, a wholesaler of drugs, and Chalen was the middleman for the heroin and cocaine, getting the product to the street after my father brought the stuff in from out of the country. I used to hear them, when I was up in the ducts, talking about the deals on the phone. The shipments. The deliveries. You needed up-front cash to play with the big overseas contacts and the *Dhavos* had that liquidity courtesy of his congregation turning their worldly goods over to him. He and Chalen had a profitable partnership until there was some kind of double cross. In retaliation, my father infiltrated Chalen's stronghold and took the one thing that male loved most. The pearl. How my father did it, I have no idea."

Duran made a fist and punched the glass, shattering the fragile barrier. Reaching in, he took the pearl and passed it over like the priceless oyster creation didn't mean anything.

And to him, she supposed, it didn't.

To her, as the cool contours of the baroque settled into the crease of her palm, she felt like she was holding her brother's life in her hand.

Not going to lose this, she thought as she tucked it into her tight sports bra.

"I think," Duran said as he inspected one of the other "windows" with his flashlight, "that my father assumed that he would kill two birds with one stone when he dropped me at Chalen's door—"

All at once, a line of light, like something you'd see at the bottom of a door, flared in the far corner. As if there were another room outside . . . and someone had just thrown a switch.

"You stay here," Duran ordered as they both wheeled in that direction and he clicked off his flashlight.

As the bedroom plunged into darkness, Ahmare didn't argue with him, although not because she had any intention of following his rules. Instead, she got her gun out again and prepared to run after him.

"Turn off your light," he whispered without looking back. "So they don't see you when I open the door. And step to the side so you stay in the shadows."

Good advice, she thought as she clicked her beam off. Best to stay hidden for as long as she could before they rushed into the other room.

To get out of the most likely path of illumination, she shuffled back a number of feet, going up against a wall. Then she held her breath as Duran got ready to open things and jump on whoever was—

Just as Duran pulled the door wide and lunged out of the bedroom, a soft sound from behind her got her attention.

She didn't have time to react. The hood that came down over her head smelled like old wool, and before she could scream, a brutally heavy hand clamped over mouth, her gun was taken, and a thick arm locked around her waist.

With brutal efficiency, she was carried off.

25

A s Duran swung the door open, he kept his body out of the way in case—
The instant he caught the scent in the air, he came alive, instincts roaring to life, possibilities filling him out from the inside. It was the same kind of rush he'd gotten from Ahmare's gift of vein, power and purpose returning.

His father was still alive.

His father was *still* in the compound.

As Duran's eyes adjusted to bright light, he

wanted to put his gun away so his attack could be more personal. But he kept the forty up in case the male was armed—although he was not worried about anyone else because there were no other scents in the air. The *Dhavos* was alone.

"Father," he said in a low growl. "Will you not welcome your son?"

Duran looked around, and instantly, nothing else mattered.

The luxurious antechamber to the *Dhavos*'s bedroom had been emptied of its fancy gilded and padded accessories. There was only one piece of furniture in it.

His *mahmen*'s cot. And on the cot . . . was a skeleton, the skull on a satin pillow, a set of clean sheets pulled up to the collarbones, a blanket folded with care over the legs. Beside the remains, on the floor, was a twisted bundle of blankets. A half-eaten tear of bread. Water bottles that bore the name "Poland Spring." A book.

Several books.

Duran stumbled across the otherwise empty space and fell to his knees at the cot. His *mahmen*'s hair . . . her long dark hair . . . had been preserved, a braid of it lying off to the side, tied with satin ribbon.

"*Mahmen*," he whispered. "I'm here. I'm going to get you out . . ."

The pits of the eye sockets stared sightlessly to the ceiling, and the jaw had been wired into place by an amateur with what looked like . . . dental floss. Dental floss had been wound around the jaw joint to keep the teeth together.

"I'm sorry, *Mahmen*." He cleared his throat. "I wasn't fast enough. I didn't get everything set fast enough. I'm so sorry."

The pain of seeing her remains and feeling his failure to save her was so great, he couldn't breathe, and then he couldn't see as tears came. Lowering his head, he tried to be as a male should, as she deserved, someone strong and capable. Someone who was worthy of the love she had so inexplicably given him.

Pulling himself together by will alone, because God knew his emotions were so big, his body could barely contain them, he sat up straight and wiped his face off on the sleeve of his shirt.

"I will get you out."

While he tried to think, he pulled the blankets higher, as if she were still alive, as if she could feel the chill in the air and he could do something to fix that. And as he did, he bumped against the cot and dislodged that which had been carefully balanced on the pillow.

The skull fell to the side, toward him, those empty sockets swinging in his direction.

Duran quickly righted his clothes and patted his hair down.

As if she could still see her precious young. Who was no longer young, regardless of what his age put him at, and who had never been precious, no matter what she had told him.

"I love you, *Mahmen*," he whispered.

He put his hand about where he imagined hers would be under the blankets, and the great divide between the living and the dead had never been so clear to him. She would never hear his words, nor he her responses. No touches. No smiles to exchange.

No future, only the past.

And there was no crossing this cavern in order to connect, at least not while he was alive, and likely not when he died, either.

After all, his father had been wrong about everything he'd told his congregation. Why wouldn't the same be true of the rumors of the Fade? The traditions of the Scribe Virgin?

You could trust no immortal leader. No temporal one, either.

Taking a deep breath, he saw the water bottles and instantly refocused.

His father was alive.

Goddamn it, the motherfucker was alive and somewhere down here.

"Ahmare," he said as he got to his feet. "Let's get you out of here with the beloved."

He needed her to be safe and on her way back to Chalen before he went after the *Dhavos*. He didn't know what kind of condition his father was in, but he couldn't take chances with Ahmare. Also didn't want to be distracted by her.

"Ahmare." She was no doubt giving him space. "You can come in."

With a frown, he looked over his shoulder toward the open door and the darkness of the bedroom. "Ahmare?"

Warning bells began to ring in his head as he flicked on his flashlight and went over to the doorway.

Before his beam had done a full sweep, he already knew she wasn't there.

"Ahmare!"

26

———◆◆◆———

AHMARE FOUGHT AGAINST HER captor with everything she had, twisting and kicking, punching—she would have brought her fangs to the party, but the sack over her head robbed her of that. Grunts, like she was taxing the male who was dragging her through a tight space, got louder.

And then he struck her hard on the side of the head and she saw stars, a whole galaxy blooming in the claustrophobic confines of the hood.

Going lax was, at first, not an option but an

overwhelming imperative, her legs falling boneless, her arms flopping loose, her mind muddling up. But as the male continued to pull her along, she saved her strength and banked on him getting sloppy with his hold.

There was a pause. Then an air lock, like they were going through a sealed portal.

Next she was thrown on the ground and something shut.

Breathing. Heavy breathing, not hers. And illumination. Through the thick hood, she could sense a light source.

When he grabbed her again, taking one of her wrists, she let loose with an attack, knowing damn well he was going to tie her up and that could not happen. Flipping around on him, she came alive and kicked up with her boot with such force, she drove the base of her spine into a hard floor and thought she had broken it in two.

But she got a clean hit on him. Had to be on his chest or the abdomen.

The impact sent him flying—he had to be airborne, given how hard he landed—and that crack? She prayed it was his head.

Ahmare moved fast, ripping the hood off and going for one of her knives—except he'd taken her weapons. Somehow, he'd stripped them off her. She must have lost consciousness.

Her eyes were momentarily blinded by the light. When that cleared, she saw a massive male coming at her, rags instead of clothes covering him, streaks of bright white down his long black hair.

He looked like Duran. An emaciated, crazed, older alter ego.

With bared fangs.

Ahmare sprang up on her feet, knowing a ground game was going to be harder for her against his weight. Settling into her thighs, she set her stance. They were in a storage area, all kinds of wooden spindle-backed chairs stacked five and six high, with conference tables lying on their sides. The lights overhead blinked like the ones out in the corridors did, the strobing effect making all movement seem stop-motion.

"My son's gotten himself a female," the *Dhavos* said. "And she is a thief. Or do you think I don't know what you took from me."

The *Dhavos* attacked her head-on, going for her throat with his hands, his arms out straight. With a duck, dodge, and spin, she slipped around behind him and shoved, giving him more momentum, creating a wave he was forced to ride even as he tried to stop himself. He hit a stack of those chairs like a bowling ball, shattering the order, pieces going flying.

He rebounded fast, jumping up on his bare feet, snapping free a chair leg that became a stake. It was some real-life Bram Stoker vampire time as he came at her again, that wooden length with its jagged, pointed end up over his shoulder.

Ahmare did him one better. She grabbed for a chair and put its four legs toward him, holding him off like a lion, redirecting his momentum again, sending him careening off to the side. His balance was bad, likely because he had been surviving on inferior blood—humans, deer—but he was motivated. Crashing into a table, he kept his weapon with him and shot back toward her.

The key was making him engage. He might have been on the thin side, but it was clear where Duran had gotten his muscularity from, and once all that meat got going, his physical strength became a weakness for her to exploit.

This time, as he lunged forth, she jumped out of his way and nailed him across the back with the chair, the force she put into the hit so great, the seat broke away from the top.

Just like the pearl popped out of her sports bra.

Chalen's beloved fell out the bottom of her windbreaker and hit the bare floor, the flash of iridescence as it ricocheted away catching her eye because she thought the *Dhavos* had somehow found a knife.

Ahmare dove for the pearl.

The *Dhavos* jumped to his feet again.

She hit the floor on a slide, her hand outstretched.

And he stabbed her.

27

------◆------

DURAN KNEW A FRESH kind of terror—which was saying a fuck of a lot—as he frantically spun his flashlight around the yes-it's-really-empty bedroom.

She wouldn't have left him. He knew that down to his soul. There was no way Ahmare would have taken the pearl and run without saying anything to him. And then he thought of the light that had come on in the antechamber—

His father. His father had turned the switch, created the distraction . . . and must have come through a hidden passageway to take her without a sound.

"Ahmare!" Duran screamed.

He picked up the first thing he came to—a bureau—and threw it across the bedroom, the wood shattering as it gouged one of the garden murals. As he yelled her name again, he wanted to trash the place, rip the drapes down, tear the bed apart, break the mirrors.

Duran forced the rage to the back of his mind because it wasn't going to help him find his female. Trying to ground himself in logic, he went back to the golden passage in case his father had entered from the rear. No scents. They hadn't gone that way so there had to be a secret access point. Focusing on the wall behind where Ahmare had been standing, he looked for a seam . . . a scratch on the floor . . . a . . .

In the mural she had been checking out right before the light had come on, there was a door depicted off to one side, as if the viewer could go through it to access another part of the fake estate.

Bringing the flashlight close to the wall, he found a faint break that followed the artist's contours of the portal, an actuality in the midst of the illusion.

Duran backed up. Took three running jumps.

And slammed his body into the "door."

The access panel gave way, the plaster that covered the wooden supports powdering under the impact, and he caught himself before he face-planted in the passageway beyond.

The scents were unmistakable. More than that, now that he was calming down, he could track Ahmare because he'd fed from her, zeroing in on her as if her body had a beacon attached to it.

She had not only come through here; she was somewhere not far.

Shining his flashlight ahead, he followed the cramped crawl space at a run and found her weapons thirty or forty feet down, the guns and knives scattered as if they had been stripped off her in a hurry. He almost left them. But as urgent as this was, he had no idea what he was going to find, so he tucked the pair of autoloaders into his belt and left the hunting knife and length of chain behind.

As he continued along, heart pounding, palms sweating, half his brain was enraged, the other terrified.

Some forty feet farther down, he came to the end of the passage, and he didn't waste time. Turning his shoulder into the solid wall, he gave himself a runway, as he had done before, and threw himself at the panel—

Like a sledgehammer hitting a steel plate, instead of breaking through, his body baseballed back, becoming airborne.

Landing on his ass, he skidded over the concrete floor, losing his flashlight, the beam of which settled at a haphazard angle focused on the panel.

Back up on his feet, he gave it a second try. And like the panel was improving its punch, he was thrown even farther, his breath getting knocked out of him as he hit the floor.

Passcode, dummy.

As he caught his breath, he saw in the beam of the flashlight that there was a passcode pad to the left, and he launched himself at it. Entering the digits, he slammed that pound key—

On the far side, he heard with his keen ears the sound of a fight.

This was good. It meant she was alive.

He shoved against the panel. Nothing gave way.

Entering the code again, he banged with his fist so she might hear that he was coming for her—

The lock did not budge. The code he had did not work.

❖

As Ahmare slid belly-down over the floor, she felt the chair leg go into the meat of her shoulder.

The penetration was so deep, her momentum stopped as the wooden stake pinned her in place to the linoleum.

Even through the pain, she stayed focused on the pearl, reaching, straining. Inches, she had only inches—

"Is that all you're after?" the *Dhavos* said through heaving breaths. "Chalen's worthless beloved?"

Thunderous impact. Over on the far wall. Like someone had hit it with their entire body.

Duran, she thought.

There was a sudden hush, as if the father had recognized the son's presence. And then . . . an inhale. A long, slow inhale.

"Dearest Virgin Scribe," the *Dhavos* whispered with reverence.

"I thought you only believed in yourself," she muttered.

Another impact, so loud she could have sworn Duran was going to come through the plaster.

"No," Duran's father said. "Your blood . . . so long it has been for me. A proper feeding . . ."

Pounding now, like Duran was hitting the other side with his fists.

"He's coming for you," she vowed grimly. "Let me go, and run for your life. I've seen what he's like when he attacks, and I promise you, you will not live through it."

The chuckle above her was evil. "I'm not worried. That's a steel door. He will not make it through—so we have plenty of time here together to get acquainted."

All at once, the stake was removed and she was freed—from the floor at least. But before she could twist around and get at him, he gripped the back of her neck and pushed down so hard, she thought her face was going to be crushed—

Sucking. On the wound.

The bastard was taking her blood.

Ahmare felt a wave of power come into her, and suddenly, it didn't matter that he was a male and he was strong and he weighed more than she did. Planting her palms, she did the push-up of all push-ups, lifting her chest and the body on top of her off the floor. So great was her anger at the taking, she got her knees up under them both as well.

And then she let out a roar and threw Duran's father off her, sending him flying into the stacks of chairs.

She was on him in a heartbeat, attacking with her own fangs, taking a hunk out of the side of his neck—except he didn't fight her. He went limp and laid himself open, his eyes rapturous as he looked at her, her reaction captivating him in an unholy way.

Yeah, she would cure him of that one.

Ahmare kneed that bastard in the nuts so hard, he sat up like a schoolboy, cupping what she'd nailed, his eyes popping from pain.

She wanted to keep going at him.

But she had to get the beloved.

Stumbling, slipping in her own blood where it had pooled on the floor, she went back to where he'd stabbed her. Where the fuck was it?

She checked over her shoulder. The *Dhavos* was where she'd left him, curled in and coughing.

Getting down on her hands and knees, she patted around the mess on the floor. It must have been kicked aside. Into the chaos of chairs.

"Goddamn it—"

The crash came from overhead, part of the ceiling breaking free, something enormous dropping through and bringing with it all kinds of ductwork.

Duran landed like a superhero, boots planted, body ready to fight, half of a section of venting falling off his huge shoulder and clanging as it hit the floor.

The sound he made was that of a T. rex, shaking the very foundation of the compound.

Behind him, his father jumped up and disappeared, leaving through a hole in the wall that appeared like a hunting dog summoned, the escape closing up in his wake as if it had never been.

"Your father!" She pointed across the room. "He went through there!"

28

DURAN'S BRAIN TOLD HIM to bolt after his father. Get his revenge. Tear the male up into pieces and eat some of them.

But his body refused to move the instant he caught the scent of Ahmare's blood in the air. "You're hurt!"

She dropped down to the ground. Like she had passed out.

"You're dying—"

"The pearl!" She looked up over her shoulder.

"I'm trying to find the beloved! It fell out while we were fighting—"

"He stabbed you!"

They were both yelling in the silence, her while she patted around, him while standing over her. And she became more frantic the more she looked without finding it while he got more enraged.

Duran knelt and captured her hands, bringing her focus to him. With a pounding heart, he measured her pupils, her skin tone, her breathing. "You're bleeding."

"I can't feel anything—"

"You're in shock—"

"I have to find the pearl!" Her voice vibrated with urgency. "I can't go back without it. Go after your father!"

Duran looked across the storage area.

A ragged path had been cut in stacks of chairs, like a body had careened through them. Streaks of red painted the floor. There was a trail of blood drops as well, one that ended at the wall.

His father. Escaping.

"Go," she said urgently. "I'll find the pearl and get out. You told me how—follow the spokes, not the curved corridors, and I have the code that works. If you go after him now, you can catch him—maybe through the ceiling again?"

He thought of his mother's bones on that cot, and the way her skull had seemed to look at him.

"Duran, go—it's what you came here to do. I'll be okay."

His eyes returned to Ahmare. Blood from that shoulder wound was dripping out the bottom of her windbreaker. What the fuck had his father stabbed her with? The hole in that light, waterproof fabric at her shoulder was too big for a dagger.

"I'll be okay," she repeated with sudden calm. Along the lines of that being the only outcome she could contemplate.

For as long as he could remember, he had always assumed his life would come down to one moment, one crucial, all-encompassing moment . . . where he plunged a knife into his father's black heart. Or snapped the male's neck. Or shot him in the face.

The method of killing didn't matter, and in his fantasies, it was often different. But that point of no return, when death took his sire unto *Dhunhd*, that was always going to be Duran's defining moment, what his life's toil boiled down to, his seminal event.

It was a shock to realize he'd been wrong about all that.

His defining moment actually came down to whether he helped a female he'd known for barely twenty-four hours . . . or left her to fulfill the destiny he had declared was his own.

It turned out to be no contest.

Duran dropped down beside her. "You search that way, I'll head over here. We're not leaving until we find the beloved."

She hesitated only a moment, but he couldn't read her expression. He was too busy patting around on the pale linoleum, trying to find a pearl that was almost the exact color of the flooring, in a room where there was debris all around and blinking fluorescent lights overhead.

He didn't think about his father. There would be time for that later.

Right now, he cared only about the pearl. Only what Ahmare needed to get her brother free.

Sweeping his vision from left to right, using his hands to feel around, he moved fast but with care, searching . . . searching . . . searching. When he came to a tossed wooden chair, he picked it up and put it behind himself. And then he arrived at a hole in the floor.

A place where something had been driven into the linoleum.

Ahmare's blood marked the point of impact. And there was more of her blood all around, already drying, making him think of the deaths in the arena. But he had to reroute from that. He needed to pull right the fuck out of thinking how she had been hurt or his head was going to explode, the tension between his love for this female and his—

His love.

For this female.

Duran glanced over at her. Her dark head was bent, her fresh blood leaving a trail even as she pressed on, her determination so fierce, he was convinced that she could lift the whole mountain they were under to locate what she was after.

He loved her. Probably since the moment she had come into that dungeon.

Take out the "probably."

The dark spices that had come out of him upon her arrival in the dungeon should have been his first clue. But whatever the increments had been, now was the realization—

With a shift in his torso, he put his hand down to catch a tilt in his weight.

A smooth nub registered under his palm.

"I got it!"

Ahmare flipped around as Duran shouted in triumph, and her wounded shoulder let out a holler—not that she cared. "Thank God!"

They met in the middle of the storage room, reaching for each other as he held the beloved between his forefinger and thumb. She kissed him without thinking, and he returned the contact without hesitation, their mouths meeting in a rush of relief.

As she pulled back, she frowned. "Why are you looking at me like that?"

Duran just stood there, staring at her. Then he seemed to snap out of whatever place he had gone to in his head and pressed the pearl into her hand. "I'll show you where to go. So I know you get out of here."

The reality that they were parting hit her as he took her over to the door. She still didn't have a solution for what was going to happen when she got back to Chalen's alone. She supposed she'd thought Duran would come with her now, and they could take down the conqueror together. But he had scores to settle here.

As she put the pearl in the pocket of her windbreaker and zipped it in, she decided Chalen was going to have to be satisfied with the beloved. And as long as she had the damn thing, she had leverage. It would have to be enough.

Before she and Duran jumped out into the corridor, he gave her her guns back, and she was glad that his father hadn't thought to strip off her ammo belt. She checked both clips and then nodded she was ready.

Duran stayed where he was for another long moment, his eyes roaming around her features. In a cold rush, she realized what he was doing.

"No," she said. "This is not the last time. Do you hear me? This is not the last time we see each other. We'll meet up . . . somehow. Somewhere. This is not it."

He took her face in his hands, his thumbs stroking her cheeks. Then he pressed his lips to hers and lingered.

Everything was said in that kiss. Although no words were spoken, everything was expressed, the yearning and the sadness, the commitment that did not include a future, the wish on both sides that it had all been different.

Their beginning, their middle, and their end.

All of it.

"Please," she whispered.

It was all the fight she could muster against an inevitability that nearly killed her. But there was no time to dwell on her emotions.

Overhead, red lights started to flash, and off in the distance, an alarm began to wail.

29

D URAN LOOKED UP AT the red lights and wanted to punch a wall. "That *sonofabitch*."

In his brain, he triangulated where they were and prayed like hell he had the storage room located right. There were a number of them in the facility—or had been twenty fucking years ago.

Grabbing Ahmare's hand, he pulled her into the corridor and broke into a flat-out run. Unlike the fluorescent tubes that had been in use constantly and were failing, the red lights, also inset into the

ceiling, were fresh as a damn daisy, no blinkers or
dead soldiers among them, their strength overpow-
ering the weaker illumination and leaving everything stained the color of blood.

Seemed fitting.

When they got to the spoke he'd been looking
for, he ran them back toward the moth room and
the entrance they'd infiltrated. And as they
pounded down the hallways side by side, he kept a
count in the back of his head. Three minutes was
nothing when your life depended on it—it was even
less when you needed to save someone else.

There was still one minute forty seconds left as
he got her back to the door they'd entered through,
the one with the code, the one he'd left open for
Chalen's guards, who had yet to materialize.

"Come with me," she said when he halted. "We'll
hunt your father together."

"That's not why I'm going back." He kissed her
hard. "I'm not leaving my mother's remains here."

"I can help!" When he shook his head, she
gripped his shoulder. "Duran, you're not going to
make it out of here alive."

He stared at her panic, at her pain, and wished
there was another fate for her, for them.

"I'm at peace with that." He searched her face for the last time. "I love you. I wish there was more for us—"

"Come with me!"

"Go! I'll find you."

It was a lie, of course. The chances of him getting to those bones and getting out in time? Less than zero—and he knew damn well she was doing that math in her head, too.

She paused for one last heartbeat. "I won't forget you. I promise."

He closed his eyes as pain lanced through him. When he reopened them, she was entering the escape tunnel.

She didn't look back and that gave him comfort. She was a fighter, and she was going to make it— and he almost pitied Chalen. The conqueror was not going to live through what that female was going to do to him.

Turning away, Duran broke out into a sprint and headed back for the *Dhavos*'s private quarters.

He couldn't leave his *mahmen*'s bones behind— even if she technically wasn't there anymore. That Fade ceremony was going to happen or he was going to die trying to get what he needed for it.

He might have sacrificed the chance to kill his father to help Ahmare.

But this was different.

———◆———

Ahmare ran through the escape tunnel like her life depended on it because duh.

And she found the first of the bodies about half-way to the vault door. It was one of Chalen's guards, curled on his side and unmoving, the scent of blood thick as if his throat had been cut.

She didn't waste any time checking into the particulars with her cell phone's light.

That alarm grew dimmer the farther she went out, but that was a function of distance, not a change in detonation. She jumped over the second of the bodies. Another guard. More blood. And a third.

The fourth was just as she came up to the vault, the robes pooled around the cooling corpse.

There was only one explanation: As Duran's father had escaped, he'd been good with a knife, even in his weakened state.

He'd also closed the heavy steel door, and her hands shook as she trained her light at the keypad and punched in the series of numbers.

And the pound key.

Ahmare's eyes were teary, and her heart was skipping beats as she prayed that the—

The rumble was dull at first. Very distant, like thunder still miles away. But the earth shook under her feet.

The explosions were starting to go off.

"Damn it! Work!" She punched in the code and hit the pound key. "Come on!"

Another rumble, more tremors, and now there were cracks and creaks in the tunnel, fine dust coming down and making her eyes sting.

"You have to work!" As she tried a third time, her eyes teared up as she remembered Duran saying the exact same thing.

But maybe those were the magic words needed because the vault lock sprang, the air lock hissed, and Ahmare yanked open the steel panel.

Bars. There were bars blocking the way out. Bars that had come down and were covered with a steel mesh that meant she could not dematerialize away.

She was trapped, either because his father had known this was the way they would try to get out, or because this was part of the doomsday scenario, a safeguard to make sure that even if the hemlock didn't work on everyone, there wouldn't be any survivors.

"No!" she screamed as part of the ceiling collapsed on her head.

30

AHMARE PULLED AGAINST THE bars. Scratched at the steel mesh. Screamed in frustration and dropped her phone because she needed both hands to try to get through the grating more than she needed illumination.

The explosions were getting closer, and the collapse that was happening deep inside the colony was creating a hot, front draft of wind that pushed against her body. The smell of gunpowder and chemicals, of electrical burn and earth, of linoleum on fire and wood as well, made her panic like an animal.

She couldn't believe this was how she was going to die. Here, in the almost-out, on the very verge of freedom and safety.

Ahmare yelled again even though there was no one to hear her, the heat making her sweat under the windbreaker, her mind splitting so that it felt as though a calm part of her was watching her struggle.

It was that section of her brain that went to her parents. Had this been what it was like for them when they'd been murdered? Had they struggled against the *lessers* as the attack happened, fighting in an untrained way against a greater, better-equipped killer, falling down, succumbing to mortal wounds . . . as a version of themselves played witness, marveling that it was happening in *this* way.

That in this particular fashion, they were leaving the earth.

Did everyone think that at the end? Especially if it was unexpected, an attack, an accident?

"Help!" she screamed—

The flare of flame on the far side of the bars came out of nowhere. One second, it was all black on the other side, her beam having settled so it faced her boots. The next, there was a very distinct, totally controlled blue flame floating in front of her.

"Get back."

The voice was female.

"Nexi?"

"No time. Get the fuck back."

The Shadow set to work on the mesh, a blowtorch eating through where the steel had been soldered into place. And all the while, the now not-so-distant explosions were going off, one by one, a drumbeat of devastation.

Ahmare yanked against the bars even though that did nothing. "Why did you come?"

"I don't know."

"You killed the guards."

"I did. But I couldn't make myself go into that compound. My body refused—besides, that was your business in there, not mine."

"Duran is still—"

"I can't think about that right now."

In the light from the sparks that kicked up where the torch was eating its way through steel, the Shadow's concentration was complete, her eyes locked on the mesh, the planes and curves of her face strobed, her hundreds of braids falling forward. She was going fast as she could.

"You're going to have to calm yourself," the female said. "I'm only going to peel back a section, we don't have time to do anything else. Close your eyes and get calm, I'll let you know when. You've got one shot."

Ahmare shut her lids tight and tried to get control of the adrenaline rushing through her veins. All she could hear was the rumbling. All she could feel was the hot breath on her back, the gust getting stronger. And now the ceiling was splintering and hitting her head and shoulders.

It reminded her of Duran crashing out of the ductwork to save her—

Calm. She needed to be calm. Calm. Calm . . .

Oreo cookies did the trick.

It should have been the Scribe Virgin, but she tried that and got nowhere. It should have been Duran's face, but that only made her want to weep. It was most certainly not the fact that he'd told her he loved her—

Had he done that? Had he really said the words—

Oreo cookies. The original ones. The old-fashioned original kind, fresh out of the blue cellophane wrapper, unrefrigerated, though some people liked them from the icebox, Oreo cookies. She pictured one in her hand and watched as her finger-tips gripped and twisted, pulling off the top, leaving her with one side that had all the frosting and one side that had just the shadow of the vanilla center.

You always ate the frosting first.

Then the two hard cracker-cookies, the one that was fresh and dry and the other that you'd had to scrape with your front teeth.

The taste was youth. And summer. And treats.

It was the contrast of the dark chocolate and the fluffy white inside—

"Now!" Nexi yelled.

Just as the corridor was crushed by thousands of pounds of dirt and rock, the mountain reclaiming the hollow spaces that had been carved out from beneath its ascent, Ahmare dematerialized her physical form and traveled in a scatter of molecules, ushered by the explosive wind, out into the night.

31

———— ✦ ————

AHMARE RE-FORMED A QUARTER of a mile away from the tunnel's cabin, and from that distance, she watched the mountain sink into itself, a great cough of dust and debris expelled over the tree line as the components of dirt, rock, and tree found a lower level. The sound was thunderous, and then there was a silence so consuming that a mosquito dive-bombing her ear was loud as a dirt bike.

She thought of the moths, now gone.

Of the skeletons, now buried.

Of Duran . . . now dead.

As the pain hit, there was a part of her that railed against having met him at all, under the guise of *Haven't I been through enough*—as if his fate had been predetermined and she could have avoided this agony now if only destiny had recognized that she'd already lost her parents, and maybe still her brother, and accordingly provided her with an alternative path to the pearl because she'd given at the office. So to speak.

But that didn't last.

Especially as she heard his voice in her head: *I don't want it to be like I never existed.*

The fact that she could be so devastated at the death of someone she hadn't even known two nights ago was a testament to the male.

"We have to get your injury fixed before we go to Chalen's."

Numbly, Ahmare looked over at Nexi, who'd rematerialized right next to her. "It's my shoulder."

There was a lame cast to her voice, and she left that right where it lay, lacking the strength to inject some show of resilience or strength. She was utterly depleted.

"Can you dematerialize back to my cabin? Do you remember where it is?" the Shadow asked.

Abruptly, Ahmare thought of the beginning of their trek through the woods, when Duran had set those two broken branches on that stump. He'd done that for her, she realized. So that she'd have a marker in case she was lost on the way back.

"He never intended to come out of there." She stared back at the collapsed mountain. "Did he."

"It's always where he was going to end." Then the Shadow added with bitterness, "Even when he was out, he never left it, and it was the only thing that ever mattered to him."

"He went back for his *mahmen*'s remains. He found them, he said."

"You didn't see them then?"

"I was busy." On that note, her head was pounding where the *Dhavos* had hit her. "And then there was no time."

"Did you get the pearl?"

In a panic, her hand slapped to the pocket she'd put it in. As soon as she felt its knobby contour, she eased up a little.

There had to be a salvaging of all this. Something good that came out of it. Otherwise, she didn't know how she was going to keep going when the sun set tomorrow or the next night or the night after that.

Too many losses. And this newest one, of a relative stranger under a mountain, for godsakes—something that seemed, in retrospect, even more unlikely than *lessers* attacking the mansion her parents worked in and killing all of the staff after the aristocrats locked them out of the safe room—compressed the time between the other deaths, making her feel as if she had lost her *mahmen* and father just the night before.

Then again, grief was not like gravity. There was no reliable law to it, no fixed rate of falling, no universal application. The only parallel was that it was everywhere and always with you to varying degrees, weighing you down.

Sometimes crushing you like a falling mountain.

Was this how Duran felt when the collapse happened on him? This suffocation, this chest pain, this pressure inside her body?

Ridiculous parallel. Because she was still breathing—which raised the question, what the hell was she going to do with the rest of her life? Vampires lived in the darkness, in the void in which humans did not tread. As she considered whatever time was left for her, long or short, the absence of sunlight she faced seemed literal and figural.

Even if she got her brother back.

It was as if Duran and what he represented to her had been all the light that had been or ever would be in her night, and now that he was eclipsed, she was relegated to permanent blindness. Memories of him took her back to when they were on the ATV, shooting through the woods. Then she was walking in the hemlocks behind him. Going down the rickety ladder, to the crawl space under the old cabin. Rushing through the tunnel, right behind him, feeling the cold and the damp, smelling the rot and the earth.

And then he was gone from those images, and she was alone in all those spaces and places . . . in the moth room, and the arena with the skeletons . . . the bedroom with the murals.

Their journey was a metaphor for life, she thought. Two people together, meeting obstacles, surmounting them. Crashing through ceilings to rescue one or the other.

She and Duran had lived a whole life together in a compressed amount of time, the entirety of a relationship laid out . . . until she was the widow at the end. And now? With his loss, she couldn't help feeling that all of the fresh air and illumination was gone from her future, any room she would ever walk into nothing but cramped and stuffy, vaguely threatening.

The magnitude of his death made her furious, not just for what she had been cheated out of, but for all of the suffering he had been born into as well.

At the hands of his father.

At the hands of . . . Chalen.

"Yes," she said grimly to the Shadow. "I remember exactly where your cabin is."

32

THIS GOES ALL THE way through."

Ahmare stared straight ahead as Nexi inspected the shoulder wound. They were back at the Shadow's cabin, with Ahmare seated on one of the rough-cut chairs, her windbreaker and shirt off, nothing but the sports bra, and the wound, and blood that was drying on her skin.

"What the hell were you stabbed with?"

"A chair leg."

The Shadow eased back. "I thought I got all of Chalen's guards."

"It was Duran's father."

"Personal attention from the *Dhavos*," Nexi muttered bitterly as she opened a medical kit. "You should be honored what with all his other priorities."

"He has no more priorities. They're all dead."

The Shadow stopped with hydrogen peroxide and gauze in her hands. Her face seemed frozen, as if whatever emotions were going through her had paralyzed her.

"What?" she said hoarsely.

"It was the end of days. They're all dead. I saw the skeletons."

The Shadow closed her eyes and shook her head. "I tried to tell them. Before I left, I tried to tell them it was all going to come to a bad end. But you cannot feed the truth to people. They have to see it themselves if they're going to."

Ahmare nodded because she agreed and because she didn't trust her voice. The sight of all those skeletons, contorted from their suffering, was one of those images she was never going to forget.

"Put this under your arm and around your back." When Ahmare just blinked at the towel, Nexi folded it a couple of times and put in place. "Hold this here so I don't get the peroxide all over everything."

"Right. Sorry."

Ahmare did as she had been told, pressing the terry cloth tight and waiting. As her eyes drifted around the cabin, she decided everything about the place should have changed. So great were the things she had gone through, she felt like everything everywhere should be as different as she was on the inside. Instead, the rough furniture and Duran's trunk and the workbench for maintaining weapons were all just where they had been left.

She focused on that trunk by the bed. Was it still full of Duran's things? Probably. And "full" was an overstatement, actually. There hadn't been much left after he'd gotten himself dressed and armed, and she thought about the clothes and personal effects that the congregation had been forced to turn in as they'd joined the cult.

Things, just things. But they were defining in a way that belied their inanimate nature. They were also a reminder, not that she needed it, that neither Duran nor the cult's followers would ever need their personal effects again.

"Brace yourself. This is going to hurt."

There was a pause, like Nexi was giving her a chance to prepare. And then the peroxide hit, cool when it was on the top of her shoulder . . . then like liquid fire as it got into the wound. Ahmare hissed and jerked forward.

"Good, now I can do the back—"

"Wait," Ahmare gritted out. "Gimme a second."

She felt as though her entire upper body on that side had been doused in gasoline and had a match tossed into the wound. As her vision blurred and she threw a hand out onto the table, a whiskey bottle appeared under her face.

"Take a swig. It'll help."

Ahmare was not a drinker, but the pain made her open to any solution. Bringing the neck up to her mouth, she took two pulls—

The coughing was *not* a help. Nope.

As her eyes watered and her shoulder screamed and her lungs issued evac orders to the Jack Daniel's that had breached their shores, Nexi sat down, like the Shadow knew it was going to be a while before they could continue with the antiseptic.

When most of the storm had cleared out, Ahmare looked at the other female. "Why did you come for us? And thank you, because I'd be dead now if you hadn't."

The Shadow took the bottle and drank like the stuff was lemonade. And if that wasn't a commentary on the difference between those who taught self-defense and those who'd actually used it, Ahmare didn't know what was.

Then again . . . she had seen real fighting now, too—and had the battle wound to show for it.

"I kept thinking about what you said," Nexi murmured. "About you killing that guy and him reaching through the divide of the raids, getting into your past, contaminating it with the stain of his blood."

Ahmare took the bottle and tried the liquor out again, going more slowly. "Little did I know what was coming next after I left his body behind."

No doubt some human had found Rollie's remains by now, but given the crew he ran with? No one would report the death.

"Your story made me think about my own childhood." The Shadow sat back, her braids falling over her muscled shoulders. "I guess I decided maybe if I came and helped you, maybe you could be the hand that reaches past my divide—only it makes things better. Like, if I saved you, maybe that'll be the good thing that changes the bad, the opposite of what happened with you."

Touched, Ahmare whispered, "I owe you my life."

The Shadow burst up as if she couldn't bear whatever she was feeling. "Or maybe I slipped and fell in the shower. Got some compassion knocked into me that's going to dissipate like a concussion as soon as I get you out of my hair."

Ahmare reached out and took Nexi's hand. "I'm sorry that you lost him, too. Duran, I mean."

The Shadow's eyes flared peridot, and given the sheen that made them glow, it was clear that under that tough exterior, there was a broken heart.

"I didn't lose him." Nexi shrugged. "The truth was, he had me. Not the other way around."

"But it's a hard death for you. Either way, it's . . . a hard death."

"They're all hard," Nexi said in a haunted voice. "Even the ones you pray for . . . are hard."

That was the last thing Ahmare heard.

Before she passed out.

33

ABOUT THREE HOURS BEFORE dawn, Ahmare approached Chalen's castle alone. She was unsteady on her feet, although that was clearing up now as she measured those stone walls—and at least she had managed to successfully dematerialize at regular intervals from Nexi's cabin to the conqueror's property. As she stopped on the far edge of the moat, she found the drawbridge up tight to the entrance, everything battened down as if an attack were expected.

She waited, her hands in her windbreaker's pockets, her chin up, her shoulder wound bandaged and strapped up under a flak shirt she'd borrowed from Nexi.

The Shadow had insisted that she take her car keys back, and she played with them under cover, running them through her fingers, the sweet chiming sound muffled.

The drawbridge lowered slowly, the clanking of the metal the big-boy magnification of what was happening in her pocket with the keys.

Two guards stepped out. The one on the right indicated the way inside.

She approached slowly, making sure to walk with no hitch in her stride. Her shoulder was a major liability in a fight, and she didn't want to give away the fact that she was injured if she could avoid it.

Her guns were tucked in under the jacket. If they wanted to pat her down and find them, fine. But last time they hadn't checked, and she hoped it would be the same now—

She passed right by the guards.

Entering the hearth room, she looked at the table and wanted to vomit. To think Duran had been on it—

"She comes back alone."

Ahmare looked over to the arch-topped door-way. Chalen was being brought in on his pallet, the four guards supporting his frail weight halting just inside the hall, their robes settling to the stone floor in folds, turning them into fluted columns.

"Where's my brother?" Ahmare demanded.

"Where's my beloved?"

She brought out the pearl, holding it between her fingertips. "I have what you want."

The decrepit male's eyes gleamed in his pitted, wrinkled face. "At last!"

"And you know why I come back alone. You know that the mountain has fallen."

"Yes, I do." Chalen was momentarily distracted from his gimmes, his cold smile revealing his bro-ken fang. "Your weapon did not survive. Pity, and we shall have to see about that."

"The hell we will."

He brushed aside her comment. "Let me have what is mine—let me have it!"

As he reached out with both clawed hands, he was a young after a toy, all greed and anticipation.

She put the pearl back in her pocket. "Where's my brother?"

Chalen's eyes narrowed and he eased back on his tufted pillow. "Where is he indeed."

Something snapped inside of Ahmare. She'd heard of people using that saying before, and now she knew what it meant.

All of a sudden, she was a different person.

She outed one of her guns without a second thought and pointed it at Chalen's head. Like it was the most natural thing in the world.

"Bring me my fucking brother right now."

"Oh, look. She has herself a weapon. I believe I told you not to bring any with you."

"Too late, motherfucker. Your guards should have patted me down when they had the chance."

"Yes." Chalen glared toward the entrance. "They should have."

"Bring me my brother, I give you the beloved."

"But what about my weapon." That smile returned. "You are not returning the weapon I gave you in good working order."

There was a whirling of metal chains and then a booming that reverberated as the drawbridge was locked up tight against the castle.

"And now, look at this," he drawled. "You're stuck inside here and you have no leverage to get yourself out."

She took the pearl back out. "Watch this."

Ahmare bent down and put the beloved on the

hard stone floor. Then she raised the steel-rein-forced tread of her boot and hovered it three inches over the invaluable object.

"You crush that," Chalen bit out, "and I will kill your brother."

"Then we have a standoff, don't we."

"No, we do not." Chalen looked toward the shadows around the now-closed entrance. "Guards!"

When there was no rush of males, no obedience, no answer, Ahmare shrugged. "I don't think they're coming. Wait—no, I'm sure of that. Sorry."

As a blood-scented breeze passed by her left ear, she smiled. Nexi had no doubt liked killing those guards. And now the Shadow was moving through the air as molecules, finding another defensible position.

"Guards!" Chalen barked. "Guards!"

"You have only four. For now."

Ahmare leveled her muzzle and pressed the trigger. The bullet went exactly where she wanted it to, into the lower leg of the front guard on the left. As the male dropped his corner of the pallet, Chalen tipped and started to fall. In a panic, he reached out and caught the edge of the pallet, his fragile body a weight he would not be able to hold for long.

The other three closed ranks, or tried to, and Ahmare picked them off, one by one, dropping them by putting bullets precisely where she needed them, in shoulders. Thighs. A foot of the one who retreated, trying to leave his master behind—

Chalen dematerialized the fuck out of there: In spite of his bad state, the old bastard was able to get himself away.

"Fuck!"

Ahmare grabbed the pearl and ran to the arch-topped doorway by the hearth—but as she did, a huge stone began rolling down, blocking the way deeper into the castle. Pulling an Indiana Jones, she slid under it in the nick of time and popped back up onto her feet.

Torches showed the way forward, but she had no clue where she was going. Her earlier trip to the lower level had not been retained as well as she'd hoped.

Nexi materialized next to her. "I found the stairs. This way."

They ran together down the stone hallway and took a couple of turns, eventually hitting a set of rough-cut steps that curved around. When they got to the bottom, there were four offshoots, four possible ways to go.

Off in the distance, there was the sound of footfalls. Many. Heavy. Coming at them.

More guards.

Ahmare knew that Chalen had gone to wherever her brother was. And might well be slaughtering Ahlan at this very second. "Damn it—"

A whistle, sharp and urgent, came from the shadows.

She and Nexi trained their guns in that direction.

A guard stepped out of the darkness with both his hands up. With his hood pulled off, his face was showing.

That young face. That red hair.

"You," Ahmare breathed. "From the forest."

It was the guard who she had spared from Duran's wrath, and Ahmare snapped ahold of Nexi's arm. "I know him. Don't shoot."

The guard looked all around, as if to make sure there was nobody other than the three of them. Then he motioned and pointed.

Ahmare glanced at Nexi. "We can trust him."

"The fuck we can—"

"I saved his life. He owes me."

The guard stamped his foot and motioned more insistently, his robe flapping. Tightening her grip on Nexi's arm, Ahmare pulled the Shadow along, and the young male led them over to a grate in the stone wall. Next thing she knew, they were crammed into a crawl space, the metal lattice closed behind them as guards flooded the area from the four corridors, congregating in the torchlight right in front of the hidden passage. Through the holes in the metal weave, Ahmare counted them. Ten. Maybe fifteen.

They were using hand signals, getting a plan.

The young guard tapped her shoulder. Nodded behind himself. And started to shuffle off in that direction.

Ahmare kept her gun out and stayed behind him, squeezing herself through a tight carve out of stone and earth that made her think of Duran's ductwork.

The young guard stopped abruptly. They had come to another grate and Ahmare pushed her way up to look through its metal links.

It was a dungeon cell, either the one Duran had been in or another just like it, bars welded into the stone floor and ceiling, a steel mesh in place, walls dripping with groundwater, bones on the floor.

There was a male curled up naked in the center of it.

"Ahlan—"

The guard covered her mouth with his hand and shook his head. Putting his forefinger to his lips, he made a *shhhh* with his mouth, and then reached for the grate, moving his fingertips around its edges as if he were looking for a release.

Ahmare did the same, even though she had no idea what she was going after. All the while, she tried to see whether her brother was breathing: Was his chest inflating at all? Was he dead? His skin was shockingly pale—white, even—

"Bring him to me!"

Chalen's voice. Off to one side. Out of range.

"I will kill him myself!"

The bars of the cell began to rise up, and guards entered, picking up her brother by the arms and starting to drag him out of view.

No! she thought as she pushed against the grating. *No!*

As Chalen barked orders, Ahlan came awake in the guards' holds, his frail body jerking, his head coming up.

"Please . . ." he said hoarsely. "No more . . . no more . . . please . . ."

Ahmare shoved the red-haired male back and got into his position. Like maybe if she tried from this angle, she could accomplish what he could not—and no, she didn't give a fuck if they were outnumbered. She had a gun. Two. Nexi also had two—

"No!" she shouted.

Her brother started to scream. And Ahmare saw that Chalen was up on his feet, shuffling over, a knife in his hand. Through the tiny holes in the grating, it was a horror movie come to life, her brother thrashing, his bony body flailing.

Ahmare started to pound on the metal lattice, but it was set so solidly into the stone, mounted so well, that there was no noise, just pain on the heels of her fists.

Chalen was laughing now, the sound loud, so loud, so evil. With maniacal eyes, he raised the blade over his head. He had both hands locked on the hilt, as if he needed the extra strength, even though the guards were holding his target still—

The crash came without warning.

From absolutely out of nowhere, the sound of something plowing into the side of the dungeon wall—or was it an explosion?—reminded Ahmare of the detonations in the mountain.

Everything stopped. Chalen. Her brother. Even the guards looked to the sound.

292 J. R. Ward

A second impact hit, and that was when the castle's side started to crumble. In response, Chalen just stood there, frozen, as if he couldn't believe someone was actually blasting through his fortification.

Except it wasn't a bomb

It was . . . an old Dodge Ram truck.

And when Ahmare saw who was behind the wheel, she swore her broken heart was playing tricks on her.

"Duran!" she yelled.

34

D URAN DIDN'T HAVE TO hit the brakes on the truck he'd stolen. All of his momentum got eaten up as he broke through into his old cell. Good thing he wore his seat belt, and thank God the airbags were broken.

He was out of that fucking Dodge in a heartbeat, and he left the engine on because he was not staying long.

Chalen's guards scattered, dropping their fragile, naked payload on the stone floor of the cell, Ahmare's brother landing in a pile of bones that surely sustained breaks.

Leading with the shotgun that had been so conveniently mounted in the cab, Duran pointed those loaded double barrels at the conqueror.

Who had pissed himself. Either because at his age he had poor bladder control or on account of the surprise.

"No one moves or I shoot your master," Duran said to the guards. "We clear?"

When there was no disagreement, he planted himself over the top of his female's brother. "Ahlan, can you get in the cab—don't fucking move, Chalen. You so much as breathe wrong and I blow your fucking balls all over the stone wall behind you."

Ahmare's brother had a good survival instinct. He picked himself up and tripped and fell his way over to the truck. The poor bastard somehow got himself in and even shut the door.

Duran took one step toward Chalen. Another. And another.

The closer he got, the more the conqueror cowered, the old male dropping the dagger, tangling in his robes, falling to the floor.

"I'll give you whatever you want," he said in a

trembling voice. Lifting his skeletal arms, he tried to protect himself. "I have money! I have—"

"Shut the fuck up. Where is Ahmare—"

There was screech of metal on metal, and then something flipped out into the cell, a grate of some kind—

The female he had come to find, the one he had refused to lose, the love of his life, burst out of the wall like she'd been shot from a cannon, her body launching at him.

"You're alive!"

Duran wanted to grab her and hold her and breathe her in, but he couldn't spare the shotgun. "We're all alive," he said as he let in a brief ray of love.

But then he nodded at Chalen. "The question is how we're going to kill this sonofabitch—wait, Nexi?"

As his old friend uncramped herself from the crawl space Ahmare had come out of, he was shocked at the Shadow's presence.

"You're always late," she muttered. "We could have used you better about ten minutes ago."

He smiled. "It's good see you, Nex."

She smiled back. "Yeah. Good to see you, too."

Ahmare was over at the truck, opening the door, checking on her brother. Hushed, hurried words between the siblings, full of gratitude and love, were a reconnection that wasn't complete yet.

Not until they were all out of here safely.

"Your guards are gone," Duran said as he looked around and realized they were alone with Chalen. "Guess they're getting reinforcements."

"I'll send them all away," the conqueror vowed. "You can go. Take her brother, you can go—"

"Shut up." Wait, there was one guard left—and he stood beside Nexi. "Who's your friend, Shadow—oh, it's you."

It was the young redhead from the forest. The one Ahmare had saved.

As the kid nodded with hesitation, like he expected to get his head blown off, Duran figured that was how Ahmare and Nexi had linked up with a hidden passageway in the castle—and why the Shadow hadn't killed that one particular guard.

"Thanks for helping my female," Duran said to the male.

Now, when the kid nodded, it was more a vow between combatants on the same side.

Ahmare came back over from the truck. "He's stable enough. But we need to get out of here."

"You have one last job." Duran held the shotgun out to her. "You get your kill. Then we go."

Without Duran's help, Ahmare thought, her brother would be dead.

Before that truck had broken through that wall, there had been no way for her to save her brother, no chance of that grate breaking free and letting her out in time.

And Chalen absolutely would have killed Ahlan. The fact that he hadn't was only because of Duran's shocking arrival. So, according to the Old Laws, and on behalf of all the others Chalen had killed in his eons as a mercenary, it was true: She could lawfully end his life.

She bent down and picked up the dagger he had been about to use. There was dried blood already on it.

Off in the distance, there was the sound of an approaching army, the guards organized and coming to save their master. But in a race against a bullet shot at point-blank range? No contest on that one. The double barrel was going to win.

"You can have your brother," Chalen said. "He's what you came for. Keep the beloved, too. I don't care. Just spare me."

Ahmare went over to the conqueror and

crouched down. The fact that he whimpered like a wounded animal made her anger worse.

"You tortured the male I loved for two decades," she gritted out. "You have killed too many to count. For godsakes, you treat your own guards like they're your property." She glanced over at the young male. "You took his voice box—"

"Who cares about them," Chalen said. "Your brother. You have your brother—"

"Take the gun and do it," Duran cut in.

But Ahmare just shook her head and looked at the young guard. "Will you help me communicate with them?"

Just as he nodded, a dozen guards arrived, bunching up in the hallway, stopping short when they saw their master was being held at gunpoint. They were fully armed themselves, but Duran shook his head at them.

"Anyone goes for a weapon, and I blow him apart. Then I'll pick you off like bottles on a fence line."

"Nexi," Ahmare said, "back the truck out and have it ready to go."

"You got it."

There was the slam of a sturdy door and the rev of a powerful engine. And then screeching and bumping as the Shadow exited the truck through the hole it had made, a shower of rocks falling as it reversed out.

Ahmare looked at the young guard, and then the others. "I want them to know that I give Chalen over to them—"

"They won't listen!" the conqueror yelled in a high, panicked voice. "I and I alone command that worthless bunch—"

"—in return for them allowing us all to leave, you included."

"Attack! Attack them!" Chalen pushed up off the floor, his horrible face flushed and sweating as he commanded his squad. "Kill them—"

"I want them to know," Ahmare continued, "that it is time they control this land, this castle. Tell them to use the gift wisely and remember what it was like to be subjugated to another."

Chalen was screaming now, his voice going hoarse, spit leaving his lips as he hollered and railed.

"Tell them this is the divide. What went before is no more. The future is theirs to command, but I will be going to Wrath and the Brotherhood. Everything needs to be lawful from now on. The laws of the King must be obeyed or the Brotherhood will mete out a punishment that will leave none alive thereafter."

The guards fired up with hand signals, and in response, the young redhead communicated with them.

She knew exactly when the message was properly received.

All of them stilled, and every single set of eyes went to Chalen.

The anger in those stares was rooted in a vengeance so deep and abiding that she knew she didn't want to see what came next.

"Come on," she said to Duran. "Let's leave them to their business."

The pair of them began backing up to the hole, and she glanced at the red-haired guard. "You're welcome to come with us—"

The young guard didn't hesitate. He walked out with them, out of the castle's lower level, into the night air . . . leaving the screams of Chalen behind.

Freedom awaited in the form of a Dodge Ram with a beautiful Shadow at the wheel and her brother alive at shotgun.

Ahmare spared her male one lingering kiss as they jumped in the truck bed. "You came back."

To her. For her.

For them.

"I decided to live in the future, not the past." Duran kissed her again and pulled the young guard up to join them. "Divides and all that."

He banged a fist into the hood of the cab, and Nexi hit the gas. As they lurched forward and had to hang on to the gunnels, she couldn't believe he'd left his *mahmen* behind.

"Those remains weren't her," he said over the din. "But my love for you? It is all of me."

35

I T WAS JUST BEFORE dawn when they finally
stopped, and Ahmare had no idea what state
they were in. They'd gone back to Nexi's cabin
for Ahmare's SUV, and there, the Shadow had
packed up some of her things and all of her weapons
and ammo. When the female had hesitated in the
doorway, they had waited as she took what seemed
like her last look around.

And then all five of them were on their way with
one last stop.

Duran returned the old truck to the yard he'd "borrowed" it from. They left the beloved in the front seat in a bright red bowl as payment for the damage to the front bumper and grill. Hopefully, the owner would sell the pearl for a big windfall.

Or maybe give it to his wife if he had one.

They went north in her SUV from there, and somewhere deep in the mountains, the Shadow had told them to take a series of turns that led them farther and farther away from the highway. Ahmare had followed directions. And now . . .

This.

As she stepped out onto the porch of a cedar house, her breath caught at that enormous view. From her vantage point overlooking the rising hills and the sleeping valleys, the very distant lights of human homes were like stars fallen from the sky.

She felt as though she had entered another world. Or awoken from a dream.

Had all of it really happened?

As she reached up to her shoulder, she winced at the shot of pain—

"Here, I made you this."

Pivoting to Duran, she stared at the plate in his hand. On it was a sandwich. Had they emptied

Nexi's refrigerator when they'd been at the Shadow's cabin? Guess they had.

He'd also brought her milk. As if she were a young heading off to school for the night.

The tears that pricked her eyes were not unexpected. And as soon as they came, he put her food down on a wooden table and came across, wrapping her up carefully on account of her shoulder wound. Her head fit perfectly on the hard pad of his pec, and behind it, beating steadily, was the heart she needed to hear.

"I thought I'd lost you," she said.

His big hand stroked up and down her good side. "I did, too."

She looked to his face. "What happened?"

Duran tucked a piece of hair behind her ear. "I did go back for my *mahmen*'s remains. But I realized, she's gone. She hasn't been here for . . . since I saw her die. What was I saving at the expense of your and my future together?"

Ahmare closed her eyes. There were no words to express how she felt, how grateful she was that he'd come to that realization, how maybe there was a life together for them after all.

"And what about your father?"

Duran took a deep breath. "I've wanted to kill

him for so long. It's been my only reason for existence, this vengeance—and you know, when I decided to let my *mahmen*'s bones go, I realized it was literally a case of my life or all that hatred. I had to release it."

"Oh, God, Duran." She shuddered against his warm body. "I'm so glad you're here and you're safe."

His hand resumed its stroking. "I got out through the old duct system, it was more efficient than running through the corridors. I broke out of an air vent with about thirty seconds to spare. I ran as fast as I could so I didn't get trapped in the collapse." His eyes traced her face. "And I knew where you would go. I returned to Chalen's as fast as I could."

"And you got there just in time."

"Almost like it was fate." He inched back and smiled down at her. "As if someone knew what they were doing all along to bring me back to you."

They both tilted their heads up and looked to the heavens. It was a beautiful night, the galaxies glowing above in the cloudless sky, the stars twinkling clearly. And yet there was also a warning to the east. A glow that was, at present, just a kindling. The fire was coming, however.

"We better go inside," she said.

On their way in, she picked up the sandwich. And he got the milk.

Teamwork, she thought, was everything in a relationship.

⸻

The house was surprisingly big, a five-bedroom place that was almost all glass on the side with the view. The interior was made up of exposed rough beams and gray slate floors, and the rustic furniture was a perfect match. Ahmare learned that the Shadow had built everything from the ground up. The female had needed to do something to keep her busy over the last twenty years, she'd told them on the trip north, and she'd taught herself construction—as well as gotten better at making tables and chairs, evidently.

As the shutters came down over all the windows and doors for the day, Duran went to have a shower and Ahmare decided to go down and check on her brother.

She found the young guard asleep sitting up in an armchair in the lower sitting area. As it was cool in the basement, she took a throw blanket and laid it over him. He woke up immediately, and she put her hand on his knee when he jerked back in surprise.

"It's okay. You're safe."

His eyes were wide and haunted, and she worried about what he saw in his dreams. She could only imagine what life had been like with Chalen, and wondered when she would learn the poor kid's story.

"You're never going back, okay?" she told him. "And we're going to take care of you."

As he exhaled in relief, she gave him a hug. And also a pillow for his head. Some night, they were going to get him into a proper bed, but she understood his need to be on guard. Who could blame him? Sometimes the worst part about trauma was not going through it. It was the aftermath, when you were free.

And you obsessed about what would have happened if you hadn't gotten out.

Heading down the hall, she was surprised to hear voices coming from Ahlan's room.

And then she stopped in his doorway. Her brother was lying back against the pillows of a queen-size bed, his gaunt face and sunken eyes still shocking to see every time she looked at him. His color was so much better, however, and he was getting bathed.

Thanks to Nexi.

The Shadow was cleaning his bruised legs with a washcloth, her braids hanging down, her hands so sure and steady. And Ahlan was staring at the female with a kind of rapturous wonder, as if he had never seen anything so beautiful in his life.

". . . even the furniture?" he was saying in a raspy voice.

"Yeah, I even made the furniture. The first couple of tries at chairs back in my cabin were not so—" Nexi glanced over to the doorway and flushed. "Oh. Hey. Figured he'd need a, you know, clean. Ing, I mean. Cleaning."

"She gave me her vein, too," Ahlan added.

"For medicinal purposes." The Shadow cleared her throat and put the washcloth she'd been using back in a stainless steel kitchen bowl she'd brought down with her. "Well, this is done. You're good. I'm going to head upstairs—"

"Will you come back," Ahlan said as he tried to sit up. "Or I can come upstairs—please."

Nexi looked down at him. She seemed surprised at the way he stared at her, and Ahmare felt a very sisterly impulse to beg the Shadow not to break his heart.

Male vampires tended to fall hard when they did.

Except then a small, secret smile graced Nexi's lips. For a split second. But it definitely was there. "Yeah. I'll be back."

When the Shadow turned to leave, her face was all composed, all hard-ass, all fighter well-trained and experienced. And Ahmare let her be with that armor.

She had seen what was behind it, however. And had a feeling that a divide had presented itself for the Shadow.

Left alone with her brother, Ahmare crossed over to the bed and sat down. His hands found hers, and they just stared at each other for the longest time.

"I'm sorry," he said. "I'm so sorry I dragged you into all this. I was so fucking stupid."

"No more of the dealing, Ahlan. Or the drugs. From here on out, you have to be clean."

"I promise."

She hoped he could keep that vow. Only time would tell, but at least the commitment was on his part at the moment.

"I miss *Mahmen* and Dad," he said. "Every night."

"Me, too."

As they both fell silent, she thought of things

she wanted to forget. Like Rollie. And Chalen's dungeon. The skeletons in that ceremonial arena and the *Dhavos*. And then, prior to all that, memories like packing up their parents' personal possessions. Shutting down the house she'd grown up in. Walking away, though she hadn't sold it yet.

Abruptly, she had no interest in ever going back to Caldwell.

"You came when I needed you," Ahlan said. "You saved me."

As he spoke, something inside her broke free—in a good way. And it was then that she realized she had always felt as though she had failed their *mahmen* and father. Somehow, in her mind, she had ascribed to herself and herself alone the ability to stop their murders. Save their lives. Restore their family to how it had been and should be.

It was craziness. But emotions were rarely logical.

But she had been able to save Ahlan—with help from Duran and Nexi. And as her brother was all she had left of her bloodline, there was peace to be had in that, peace that ushered in a whole lot of forgiveness for those things she had felt responsible for, even if she could not control them.

Ahmare stared into eyes that were the same color as her own. And thought more of the divides in people's lives, the starts and finishes of stages, the eras that you weren't aware of being in . . . until they were over.

"Do you want to leave Caldwell?" she asked.

"Yes," her brother said, "I do."

36

IT REALLY SHOULDN'T BE that tough.

As Duran faced off at the shower, he stared at the faucet handle like it held the key to the mysteries of the universe: H vs. C. His choice of one or the other seemed monumental. A predictor of things to come. A prognostication as to whether what was going to come next in his life would be good . . . or bad.

Reaching into the tiled alcove, he started the water and moved the handle to the "C" position—

and was disappointed in himself as he pulled the curtain back into place. But there was no reason to think he'd tolerate warmth any better now than he'd handled it back at Nexi's cabin. Had that been two nights ago? Or . . . only one?

Time had little meaning to him. Everything had been so momentous that measuring things in terms of twenty-four hour clips seemed like using a beach to count grains of sand.

Getting out of his filthy, dirty, sweat- and blood-stained clothes, he looked down at his body. There were bruises on his skin. Scrapes that were leaking. Cuts that were healing already.

Thanks to Ahmare's vein.

There were a lot of other things that were thanks to her. He touched his neck, which was, for the first time in twenty years, free of a shock collar. She had even been the one to cut the thing off him, sawing through that which had been locked on his throat by Chalen.

Who most certainly was no longer on the planet.

Ahmare had freed him in so many ways. Yet he was worried there were things even she couldn't let him out of.

He drew the shower curtain back again. As he

pictured Ahmare's face when she had broken out of that crawl space in the cell and thrown herself at him, he focused on the faucet's "H."

Start as you mean to go on, he told himself as he leaned in and moved the handle up . . . up . . . up.

The change in temperature came slowly, the hot water routed up from some kind of heater somewhere. But soon, the spray was kicking out warmth.

He braced himself as he stepped under.

The rush as it hit his head made him shudder, but not because it was unpleasant. It was because his body was unused to anything other than discomfort, like his nerves had been re-programmed and if shit didn't hurt, it didn't feel right.

He told himself he was going to get used to the new way. The normal way. The . . . better way.

When he wasn't sure he believed that, he went for the soap and cleaned himself, suds sluicing down his chest, his sex, his thighs. He was tired. His back hurt. One knee felt like it wanted to bend backward.

Shouldn't this be a time for rejoicing? he thought.

"Mind if I join you?"

He whipped the curtain back. Ahmare was naked, her clothes pooled where he'd left his own, her hair freed from her ponytail. She, too, had bruises, on the side of her face. Her arm. Her hip. And then there was that shoulder wound.

"Please, God, yes, please," he breathed.

She smiled a little and then turned to the mirror. After wiping the glass off with her hand, she picked the adhesive off the bandage around her shoulder. As she peeled the gauze free, he winced. The ragged, two-sided wound was healing, but it was angry red, with jagged edges and a very deep core.

He thought of the mark in the linoleum on that floor, when he had been searching with her for the pearl.

"My father . . ." He couldn't finish as rage rekindled.

"It doesn't matter now."

With the urge to kill surging in him, he tried to put the aggression aside. "Are you sure you want to get that wet?"

"It's closed."

She turned to him and his eyes went to her breasts. Her waist. Her hips.

"Come under the warm water," he beckoned.

Ahmare took his hand, and as he drew her up against him, his body responded, thickening, lengthening. Where it counted.

Tasting her mouth under the falling spray, he

was hungry, but he was careful as he held her close and ran his hands up and down her body. Tongues, languid and hot, penetrated and slid as she fit herself against him, her breasts pushing into the wall of his chest.

He washed her as a way to honor her, shampooing her long hair, soaping her body, taking his time as he kissed and licked . . . everywhere. Especially between her legs. She ended up sitting on the ledge in the corner, her thighs split to his hungry, unknowledgeable tongue. He'd never done anything like this before, some inner drive guiding him. He must be doing something right, though.

She orgasmed against his lips, and he drank of her.

Rising up on his knees, he angled himself in the way she had done when they'd first been together.

He looked into her eyes as he entered her.

But even as he gasped at the hold, he stopped himself. Cradling the back of her head, he bared his throat to her.

"Take from me," he said in a guttural voice. "Let me make you strong."

⬦

Ahmare's fangs descended in a rush, and yet she was too stunned to move. Duran, after all he had been through, was giving himself to her in the most complete of ways, and she was so struck by the gift, she could only blink away tears.

As she stared at him, she couldn't stop picturing him as he had emerged from the water falling in that dungeon, the rush split by his huge shoulders, his magnificent body so proud and strong even in his captivity. And now here they were, in a warm shower together, in a safe house.

With a different kind of water falling.

Slipping her hand around the back of his neck, she drew him toward her. She pressed her lips to the thick vein that roped up the side of his throat, and then she ran one fang up his flesh. As he shuddered beneath the contact, she tilted her pelvis and reached down, clamping a hand on his ass and pulling him into her.

She struck as he gasped again at their joining.

His blood was a roar in her mouth, his arousal a hot brand in her sex, his body a blanket of strength against her own. She'd had no idea she was starving until she tasted him, and then suddenly she was ravenous.

As she took from him, he took her, penetrating and retreating, finding a rhythm.

The release that wracked her was so intense, she

worried she was chewing him raw, but he didn't seem to care. He was wild, too, his head back, his throat exposed, his hips pumping.

For a moment, she was worried that he would need pain to find his climax, as he had back in that bolt-hole they'd spent their first day in—and watching him hurt himself to get to a point of pleasure had been hard enough to witness before. Now? With everything she felt for him and all they had been through, it would kill her.

But he had no problem. With a shout of her name, he soared, clearly free of the burdens he had carried, and tears of joy came to her eyes. So natural. So right—for the both of them: He was down the back of her throat, in her gut, in her body, coming in great kicks into her sex. Duran . . . was everywhere and everything, all she knew, all she needed.

And it was beautiful.

So much so, she might well drain him dry if she took too much—and so she was careful to force herself to release his vein way before she was satiated, her love for him greater than her greed for his blood. Licking the puncture wounds closed, she slumped against the wall and propped her heels on the ledge, opening herself up as wide as she could.

Duran planted his palms on the tile wall, his

great arms bowing out, and then he got to the grind, his abs rolling under his tight skin, his hips working, his lips finding hers until the rhythm got too intense. Looking down her body, beneath her breasts, she watched him go in and out of her, the sight so erotic, she came again.

And again.

And . . . again.

He was filling her up on the inside once more, marking her as males did when they had bonded, mating her in the rawest sense of the word. His face, as he strained and powered over her, was intense, his eyes glowing, his fangs bared as his lips curled off his canines in pleasure.

He was the most beautiful thing she'd ever seen.

And he was alive.

When he finally stilled, she was boneless and fully satisfied. And if, tomorrow night, she had to add stiffness between her legs to her legion of bumps and bruises?

Well worth it. Sooooooo worth it.

"You ready for bed?" he asked with a slow smile.

"Beyond ready." She brushed his wet hair back from his forehead. "I can't wait to sleep all day long."

"If I happen to wake you," he drawled as he bent

to one of her breasts and sucked her nipple between his lips, "I want to apologize in advance."

"Do not hesitate to disturb my sleep with the likes of this," she groaned as he nuzzled against her.

Out of the shower, they dried off and went to fall into the big queen-size bed that was covered with quilts. Their room was in the back of the house on the first floor, and she had an idea, considering what had happened in the shower, of why Nexi had given them this particular locale.

Far from the basement.

So no one would hear . . . things.

There was no reason to wear nightclothes, not that they had much to change into—and funny how none of that mattered. After everything they had been through, things like changes of socks and clean underwear were way down the list of urgent priorities. Undoubtedly, this would recalibrate, however.

At least, she hoped it did.

"I look forward to normal," she said as she nestled in against him. "To First Meal with you. Last Meal with you. Nightly habits are such a blessing."

As he kissed her on the top of the head, she heard him mumble something. She yawned. Winced as she shifted and her shoulder protested. Knew that the feeding she'd just had would take her light-years ahead in her healing.

"I love you," she said.

"I love you, too," Duran returned.

There was a strange tension in his voice, one that made her nervous on some deep level even as she told herself not to worry about it. And then her body's need for rest overrode her mind's warning system, sleep arriving and slamming the door on the external world.

Subsuming her in a glorious float.

Where, for once, there were no bad dreams.

37

DURAN DIDN'T SLEEP.

Even though he was beyond exhausted, he could not let go of consciousness, no matter how many times he closed his eyes and resolved to follow Ahmare's excellent example.

Sometime around three in the afternoon, he told himself it was because his body was one giant contusion. He told himself the insomnia was also because he was in a strange house. And finally, he told himself it was excitement over the future, over his love with Ahmare . . . over the fact that against the odds, he'd finally escaped Chalen's hold.

Freedom, after all, was heady stuff. And that was before you tacked on two decades of having been tortured.

By the time the sun dropped below the horizon, however, he knew none of that was the problem.

Inside his soul, something vital was screaming, the terrible energy emanating from the center of his chest and contaminating all of him. His love for Ahmare was great enough to make him want to stay with her in spite of the agitation.

But in the end, he got out of bed.

Duran moved slowly so as not to disturb her, although he feared the "why" behind the respect he paid to her slumber. He found some clothes hanging in the closet, ones that were not his own but that fit his body—to the point where he wondered if Nexi hadn't hoped the pair of them would end up here in this safe house.

Dressed and standing over the bed, he stared down at Ahmare, watching her move into the warm spot he'd left under the covers. Her face was tucked into the blankets, her dark lashes on her cheeks, her hair on the pillow where he had laid his head. In her repose, she seemed innocent and young, something to be protected.

And here he was, resolving to leave her.

As he turned away, he felt like death had come to him once more. And this time, it would not be denied.

The next thing he knew, he was standing in front of the big door of the mountain house. He had no idea how he had come to be there, what commands he had given his body, what plan he had for where he was going.

All he knew was that he was—

"Do *not* tell me you're leaving her."

Twisting around, he looked at Nexi, who had mounted the open stairs coming up from the basement. The Shadow's deep-set eyes were accusatory. Her tone was worse.

Duran refocused on the door. "He's inside me, too."

"What the hell are you talking about." The Shadow came around and put herself in between him and the exit. "Your sire?"

"You know what he did to my *mahmen*."

"And you think you're going to pull that shit on Ahmare? Come on." Nexi crossed her arms over her chest and lifted her chin. "You've done nothing but try to save people. Your *mahmen*. Me. Ahmare and her brother. You do not have to worry about turning into your father just because you're in love."

He focused on the Shadow properly instead of looking over her shoulder at the door. "I'm sorry. For hurting you. I know I did, and I shouldn't have."

Nexi glanced away. Then shrugged. "It is what it is. You know, two decades ago, when I was getting out of the colony . . . I wasn't in the right place for a relationship anyway. I was knee-deep in all kinds of bad thoughts and bad patterns. Who knows what I actually felt for you. I thought it was love. Maybe it was more like relief and grief coupled with a terror of being alone."

"I should have said something. To let you know . . ."

"What, that you weren't available? I knew that, and I cared anyway. Words don't change emotions. Time does."

"I'm still sorry."

"Good. I'm glad. Now don't fuck things up with that female just because you're running again. The mountain is down. Ahmare said they all died. It's over."

"I think my father ended everything right after

my *mahmen* died and he gave me to Chalen. The bodies had decomposed entirely. Only bones were left."

"He was straight-up evil."

"I want to kill him."

"Is that where you're going with all those weapons?"

Duran looked down at himself and was surprised to find that he had not only clothed himself but also strapped on all his guns and ammo. "I don't know where I'm going and that's the truth."

"What did you tell Ahmare?"

"Nothing. She's asleep."

"You're a coward then."

"I didn't *ahvenge* my *mahmen*, after all. And my father is likely dead somewhere under that mountain. I have no future—"

"Oh, cut the shit. Of course you have a future. It's every time you look at that female. And she feels the same for you. God knows I'm no expert in romance, but come on. Even I see it."

"Are you going to stop me? Is that why you're blocking the door?"

There was a long silence. Then Nexi got out of his way, standing off to the side. "What do you want me to tell her?"

"I'll be back. I'm just going for a walk to clear my head."

"You sure about that?"

No. "Yes."

"Fair enough. I'll tell her you went for a walk. But FYI, I saw what losing you did to her once. I'd appreciate you not putting me or a decent female like that back in that place. It's a shitty thing to do, and with both your parents dead now, it's about damn time you start leading your own life. You don't owe anybody anything—except that female you're walking out on."

As Nexi went past him to go back down to the basement, she gave him a quick, hard hug. "You don't deserve all the pain you've had. A lot of it wasn't anything to do with you and it is certainly nothing to fault yourself for. But this? Leaving now? You're being your own enemy, creating your own prison, and after all the time you've been in dungeons created by other people, haven't you had enough of that shit?"

Left alone, Duran stayed where he was, on the precipice . . . for a while. Then he unlocked the door and stepped out onto the stoop. The air was cool and cleaner at this altitude, the scent of the pines that grew all around the house thick in the night.

His feet started moving, his boots making no sound.

Because he didn't want anyone to hear his departure.

Least of all his Ahmare.

38

AHMARE BOLTED UPRIGHT IN bed, heart hammering in her chest, breath sawing down her throat. Putting her hand up to her sternum, she looked around.

Duran was gone.

And not in-the-bathroom gone.

As in all-weapons-that-had-been-on-the-bureau gone.

Jumping from the bed, she nearly bolted naked out of their room, but managed at the last moment to pull on a robe that hung on the back of the door.

The house was quiet. The shutters still down. No one—

The scent of bacon drifted into her nose and she exhaled in relief. Telling herself not to be so paranoid, she forced herself to walk like a normal, sane person down to the kitchen . . . where she found Nexi facing the stove, cooking up some strips of heaven in a pan.

Ahmare tried not to rush to conclusions when Duran was nowhere to be found in the galley.

"I guess I slept in," she said in what she hoped was a calm, conversational tone.

In her head, she was screaming, *WHERE IS HE!*

"Mattress okay for you then?" the Shadow murmured.

"Oh, yes. Thank you."

When Nexi didn't turn around, when she just poked at the sizzling maple-smoked bacon in the pan with a fork, the pain in Ahmare's chest came back.

"When did he leave?" she asked baldly.

"Fifteen minutes ago. Twenty at the most."

Ahmare stumbled over and took a stool. "He didn't wake me."

"I told him not to go." The Shadow finally pivoted around, crossing her arms, that fork sticking out of her fist. "I told him he was an asshole. Look, he's been through a lot. You can't imagine what it was like in the colony with his father. What happened there. Even if he told you some of it, he didn't tell you everything, and then there was Chalen. It's too much to hold in one male's head." Nexi touched her temple. "Too much to hold in anyone's head. He loves you. He just needs time. He doesn't know who he is right now. He'll be back, though."

"How can you be sure?"

"He's bonded with you," the Shadow said wryly. "Or do you think that's cologne he's sprayed himself with?"

Ahmare thought about the compression of hours. And her sense that she had known these people her entire life when in fact that was only true about her brother downstairs.

"How is Ahlan?" she asked roughly.

"Great. I mean—he's recovering. He's asleep. I mean, I checked on him—"

"It's okay." Ahmare tried to smile through the agony in her heart. "I think I know where it's going between the two of you. My brother can be a lot to deal with, but something tells me you can handle him."

The Shadow smiled a little and turned back to the bacon, flipping the strips over one by one. "You better believe I can."

Ahmare got off the stool, pushing it back under the counter. Then she cleared her throat and started to make some excuse about returning to her bedroom—

"He's going to be back." Nexi looked over her shoulder. "But he has unfinished business, business that will never be finished. There's a reason why people *ahvenge* their dead. It's a brutal way of dealing with grief, but the shit works."

"Do you think his father died in the mountain's collapse?"

"I didn't see him. You did. What do you think?"

"I don't know. I really don't."

———◆———

Back in their bedroom, Ahmare plumped up the pillows and propped herself against the headboard. Tucking her knees into her chest, she stared across at the bureau on which Duran's weapons had been laid.

Like if she kept looking over there, they would mysteriously reappear and mean that he was still in bed with her.

Intellectually, she knew what the Shadow had said made sense. After her parents had been killed, she had roamed the nights, all pent-up anger and aggression with no target for her to take her emotions out on.

She'd even gone so far as to try and hunt *lessers* in the alleyways of Caldwell. As if she knew what she was doing, as if she were a member of the Brotherhood. So stupid and dangerous. But her grief and rage had been so great that her body had been a bowl overflowing, the container of her skin insufficient to hold all that consumed her.

She knew exactly how Duran felt.

And she told herself she had to believe in what they had. But that now sounded ridiculous. They were on, what, night three of a relationship now?

Anger swelled in the midst of her sadness as she remembered what his father had looked like, the crazy eyes, the long, white-streaked hair, the greedy way he'd stared at her.

The automatic shutters began to lift, the daytime panels retracting slowly from the glass on the exterior as they rolled into their storage units at the top of the headers.

She looked over to the window. As she'd left the lights off, she could see clearly into the distance, to the wide mountain-valley view that seemed to suggest all corners of the world could be seen—

A figure was right at her window.

And the hulking form was revealed inch by inch by the rising shutter.

She knew who it was before she saw all of him, and she jumped back in the sheets.

Duran's father was standing just outside the glass, sure as if she had conjured him with her memories, a spectral manifestation of the loathing she felt for him.

Except this was not a ghost.

As the moonlight shone down on his white-streaked hair, his eyes glinted in a nasty way. And with a smile of pure evil, he bared his fangs and pointed at her with a knife that gleamed.

Ahmare turned and lunged for the gun she'd put on the bedside.

When she wheeled around, she brought the muzzle up with her to shoot.

She did not pull the trigger.

No reason to.

Directly behind the male, materializing like the Grim Reaper, Duran's larger body appeared from out of the shadows. He was enormous behind his father, his arms hanging with menace, his head tilted down.

Her male had not left her as it turned out.

And he was going to settle all scores.

Ahmare lowered her gun. The *Dhavos* was so fixated on her, he didn't even sense what was upon him. But that was going to be an issue fixed all too soon.

Shifting off the bed, she approached the window, and Duran's father seemed to take this as an invitation, his nose flaring as if he were trying to scent her through the glass.

His face was rapt, his eyes obsessed.

Grasping the edge of the heavy curtain, Ahmare drew the folds of fabric across the glass to block the view. She was halfway to home when the *Dhavos* frowned and tilted his head. Then he turned around—

His scream was muffled.

And then there were many others.

With the drapes shut, Ahmare tightened the sash on her robe and walked calmly out of the bedroom.

She was waiting for her male when the front door to the house swung wide.

Duran was breathing heavily, and blood ran down his chin, dropped off his fingers, and stained all of his clothes.

His eyes, as they met hers, were wary, as if he didn't know what kind of reception he was going to get.

Ahmare opened her arms. "Come here, my love. Let me hold you."

Duran stumbled across the slate floor and fell against her. As great sobs came out of him and his legs buckled, she eased him down and arranged him in her lap. Covering him with her body, sheltering him with her love, she murmured in his ear.

Telling him, and believing it, that the score had been evened. The end had come.

And that he was the very best son to his *mahmen* that any male could ever be.

EPILOGUE

Six Months Later . . .

I CAN'T BELIEVE THIS IS OURS," Ahmare said as she and Nexi walked into the gym. The space was ten thousand square feet of treadmills, ellipticals, weights, and machines. There were two studios, as well, one for aerobics and one for spin classes, and also offices for the personal trainers and full showers and locker rooms for members.

"Big opening tomorrow." Nexi put her palm out. "Put 'er here, partner."

Ahmare smacked palms and then smiled at Rudie. "Hey, you ready?"

Rudie, the young redheaded guard, had taken to office management like a pro. With an automated speech machine, he could communicate with all their employees, and it was good to see his shy personality shine.

He'd certainly earned the happiness.

"I brought us something to celebrate with." Ahmare nodded toward the staff break room. "Where are the boys, though?"

Duran—who was now going by the name Theo, a change that had been deliberate on his part and easy for everyone else to make—and Ahlan came in right on cue, bunches of helium balloons bobbing over their heads, the broad smiles of bonded males on their faces.

Theo, Ahmare reflected as she smiled at her mate, was a great name for a great male. And what a wonderful way to honor his *mahmen*.

And that wasn't the only thing that was new to him. After he'd spent a lifetime in the cult and then as a prisoner, she'd had some concerns about how he would adjust to the modern world, and she was relieved that he was doing really well. He liked Netflix, Starbucks, and Instagram. He wasn't so crazy for the noises and traffic of Caldwell, and he was suspicious of the number of humans that seemed to him to be everywhere. But on the whole, he was doing great.

So was her brother.

Ahlan went up and kissed Nexi on the mouth, bending her body backward and whispering things that were no doubt fit only for the Shadow's ears.

Theo held out a set of balloons that . . . had marker over them. "I had to cross out the 'boy' and work some magic."

Ahmare laughed. Each one of the balloons had "Atta GIRL" on them, and she could only imagine the care he'd taken to correct the sexism.

"Thank you, they're beautiful," she said as she put her arms around him and they lingered over a kiss. "And I'm going to show you my gratitude later tonight."

"Can I go buy more balloons right now?"

Fitting herself under his arm, she pulled him in tight, and the five of them walked back to the break room. Various opening-night issues needed to be discussed, and Rudie's electronic voice as he started down the list was as natural-sounding as anyone else's as far as the group was concerned.

They had bought the gym thanks to Chalen's $276,457.

Ahlan had presented the cash to the group after he and Ahmare had gone up to Caldwell to move out about two weeks after the drama was over. And when Ahmare had suggested she and Nexi go in on a gym that focused on self-defense for vampire females, the Shadow had thought that was a great idea. After all, vampires could dematerialize from all over. And there were a lot of females who didn't feel safe in the world after the raids.

Ahmare and Nexi were going to change that, and even Wrath and the Brotherhood had come down and inspected things, excited about the good work they were going to do.

Ahmare went to the cupboard and took out—

"Oreos?" Nexi said. "Oreos."

"You hate kale and you know it," she said to her partner. "And this is a celebration."

Ahmare opened the package and slid the tray full of chocolate-and-vanilla goodness out. She offered them to Nexi and Ahlan and Rudie. When she came up to her Theo, his smile was wide, but his eyes were serious.

He knew about the why of this, and it was not just because Oreos were awesome. She'd told him about Nexi and the blowtorch, the seconds only to spare, the almost not-out.

Her life saved by Nabisco, as it were.

They'd talked a lot about the past over the months since they'd moved into Nexi's safe house, both the events of those fateful three nights that had started with her first contact with Chalen, and the things that had come before, her family, his *mahmen*, the raids, the colony.

What he had done to his father outside their room.

They were both healing, and so were the others. There was a lot more distance to cover, but happiness was a great antiseptic to the wounds inside the soul, and there were all kinds of goodness and support inside that mountain house where they all lived.

Putting her cookie out, she said, "Cheers, to us."

"To us," they all murmured, Oreos meeting in the center as if they were glasses.

And then everyone ate theirs their own way. Theo and Ahmare were twist-and-splitters. Nexi ate hers in three bites. Ahlan put his in his piehole on a oner. And Rudie bit the top of his cookie off, using his fangs like they were surgical knives.

It didn't matter how you ate your cookie, after all.

As long as you had family to share it with.

ACKNOWLEDGMENTS

With so many thanks to readers far and wide. Thank you also to Meg Ruley and everyone at JRA, and with so much gratitude to Lauren McKenna and Jennifer Bergstrom and everyone at Gallery Books and Simon & Schuster!

As always, with thanks to Team Waud and my family, both of blood and adoption.

Oh, and this wouldn't have been possible without the talents and dedication of WriterDog!

Turn the page for a sneak peek of

THE

JACKAL

the first book in J. R. Ward's new spinoff series

BLACK DAGGER BROTHERHOOD:
PRISON CAMP

Chapter One

THE WHOLE "LIFE IS a highway" meta-phor was so ubiquitous, so over-used, so threadbare and torn-patched, that as Nyx sat in the passenger side of a ten-year-old station wagon and stared at the moonlit asphalt trail cutting through brush and bramble in western New York State, she wasn't thinking a damn thing about how similar the course of roads and lives could be: Cool-coasting stretches of normal, speed limit driving. Sweet-sailing easy declines of coasting. Bad, bumpy, rough patches that rattled your teeth and made you reconsider whether you wanted to be in a car at all. Uphill hauls that you thought would never end.

And then there were the obstacles, the ones that came from out of nowhere and carried you so far off the planned trip, you ended up in a completely different place.

Some of these had four legs and a kid named Bambi, for example.

"Watch out!" Nyx yelled as she clapped a hand on the steering wheel and took control.

Too late. Over the screeching of tires, the impact was sickeningly soft, the kind of thing that happened when steel hit flesh, and her sister's response was to cover her eyes and tuck in her knees.

Not helpful considering Posie was the one with the access to the brake pedal. But also completely in the younger female's character.

The station wagon, being an inanimate object set into motion, had no brain of its own, but plenty of motivation from the sixty-two miles an hour they had been going. As such, the old Volvo went bucking bronco as they veered off of the rural byway, momentum heaving its stiff, cumbersome body into a series of hill-and-dale dance moves that had Nyx hitting her head on the padded roof even though she was belted in.

And in another life/highway parallel, this time, she saw what was coming. The headlights strobed what was in front of the car, the beams point-and-shooting in whatever direction and angle the front grill happened to be thrown in. For the most part, there was just a leafy morass of bushes on the up-and-come, the green spongy territory a far better outcome than she would have predicted.

That did not last.

Like a creature rising out of the depths of a lake, something brown, thick, and vertical was teased in the verdant light show, appearing and disappearing as the shafts of illumination willy'd their nilly around. It was a threat that, at first, she wasn't sure she was seeing.

But no. It was a tree. And not only was the arbo-real surprise an immovable object, it was as if a steel crank-chain ran between its thick trunk and the undercarriage of the station wagon.

If you'd steered for a collision course, you couldn't have done a better job.

Inevitable covered it.

Nyx's only thought was for her sister. Posie had focused ahead and was braced in the driver's seat, her arms straight out, fingers splayed, like she was going to try to push the tree away—

The impact was like being punched all over the body, and there must have been a crunch of metal meeting wood, but with the air bags deploying and the ringing in Nyx's ears, she couldn't hear much. Couldn't breathe. Couldn't seem to see.

Hissing. Dripping. Burned rubber and something chemical in her nose.

Someone was coughing. Her? She couldn't be sure.

"Posie?"

"I'm okay, I'm okay . . ."

Nyx rubbed her stinging eyes and coughed. Fumbling for the door handle, she popped the release and shoved hard against some kind of resistance. "I'm coming around to help you out."

Assuming she could get out of the damn car herself.

Putting her shoulder into the effort, she forced the door panel through some fluffy and green, and the payback was that the bush barged in, expanding into the car like a dog that wanted to sniff around.

She fell out of her seat and rolled onto scruff. All-fouring it for a spell, she managed to get up on to her feet, and steady herself on the car's quarter panels as she went around to the driver's side. Peeling open Posie's, door, she leaned in and released the seat belt.

"I got you," she grunted as she dragged her sister out.

Pushing Posie against the car, she cleared the blond hair back from those soft features. No blood. No glass in the perfect skin. Nose was still straight as a pin.

"You're okay," Nyx announced. Because she needed to believe it.

"What about the deer?"

Nyx kept the curses to herself. They were about ten miles from home, and what mattered was whether the car was drivable. No offense to Mother Nature and animal lovers anywhere, but that four-legged scourge of the interstate was low on the list of priorities.

Stumbling to the front, she shook her head at the damage. A good two feet of the hood—and therefore, the engine—was compressed around a trunk that had all the flexibility of an I-beam, and she was hardly an automotive expert, but this had to be incompatible with vroom-vroom, home safe.

"Shit," she breathed.

"What about the deer?"

Closing her eyes, she reminded herself of the birth order. She was the older responsible one, black-haired and brusque like their father had been. Posie was the blond-haired, good-hearted youngest, with all the warmth and sunny nature that their *mahmen* had sported.

And the middle?

She couldn't go down the Janelle rabbit hole right now.

Back over at her own open door, Nyx leaned in and moved the deflated air bag out of the way. Where was her phone? She'd put it in a drink cup holder after she'd texted their grandfather when they'd left the Hannaford.

Clearly, another casualty of $e = mc^2$.

Bracing her hand on the seat, she leaned down into the wheel well and—got it.

"Ahh . . . damn it."

The screen was cracked and the unit dark. When she tried to fire the thing up, it was a no go. Straightening, she looked across the ruined hood. "Posie, where is your—"

"What?" Her sister had turned away from the wreck, her eyes focused on the road that was a good fifty yards away, her stick-straight hair tangled down her back. "Huh?"

"Your phone. Where is it?"

Posie looked over her shoulder. "I left it at home. You had yours so I just, you know."

Great. "You need to dematerialize back to the farmhouse. Tell grandfather to bring the tow truck and—"

"I'm not leaving here until we take care of the deer."

"Posie, this is a human road and—"

"It is suffering!" Tears glistened in those morning glory blue eyes. "And just because it's an animal doesn't mean its life doesn't matter."

"Okay. I need you to snap out of that." Nyx glared across the steaming mess. "We have to solve this problem now—"

"I'm not leaving until—"

"—because we have two hundred dollars of groceries melting in the back. We cannot afford to lose a week's worth of—"

"—we take care of that poor animal."

Nyx swung her eyes away from her sister, the crash, the problem she had to fix so goddamn Posie could continue to give her heart out to the world, and worry about things other than how to pay the rent, keep food on the table, and make sure they had electricity.

When she trusted herself to look back without hurling a bunch of be-practical f-bombs at her fricking sister, she saw absolutely no change in Posie's resolve. And this was the problem. A sweet nature, yes. That annoying, bleeding heart, empathic bullcrap, yes. Iron will? When it came down to it, and at the most inopportune times, check.

That female was not budging on the deer-thing.

Nyx threw up her hands, cursed—loudly—and gave in.

Back in the car. Opening the glove box. Taking out the nine-millimeter handgun she took with her everywhere. Because that's what you did when you were a vampire living in a world that had *lessers* and humans in it.

As she came around the rear of the station wagon, she looked through the back window and eyed the reusable grocery bags. They were crammed up against the bench seat as a result of the crash, and it was a good news/bad news situation. Anything breakable was done for, but at least the cold items were cloistered together, united in a fight against the eighty-degree August night.

"Oh, thank you, Nyx." Posie rushed forward. "We'll help the—wait, what are you doing with a gun?"

Nyx didn't pause as she passed by, so Posie grabbed her arm. "Why do you have the gun?"

"What do you think I'm going to do to the damn thing? CPR?"

Posie threw out her anchor again. "No! We need to help it—"

Nyx put her face into her sister's and spoke in a dead tone. "If it's suffering, I'm going to put it down. It's the right thing to do. That *is* the way I will help it."

Her sister's hands went to her face, pressing into horrified cheeks. "It's my fault. I hit the deer."

"It was an accident." Nyx turned her sister around to face the station wagon. "Stay here and don't look. I'll take care of it."

"I didn't mean to hurt the—"

"You're the last person on the planet who'd intentionally hurt anything. Now stay the hell here."

The sound of Posie softly crying escorted Nyx back toward the road, haunting her as she followed the tire gouges in the dirt and the path through ruined foliage. She found the deer about fifteen feet away from where they'd veered off—

Nyx stopped dead in her tracks. Blinked a couple of times.

Considered vomiting.

It wasn't a deer.

Those were arms. And legs. Thin ones, granted, and covered with fawn-colored clothes that were in rags. But nothing about what had been struck was animal in nature. Worse? The scent of the blood that had been spilled was not human.

It was a vampire.

They'd hit one of their own.

Nyx ran over to the body, put the gun away, and kneeled down. "Are you okay?"

Dumbass question. But the sound of her voice roused the injured, a pasty face turning toward her.

It was a male. A pretrans male. And oh, God, the whites of both his eyes had gone red, although she couldn't tell whether it was because of the blood running down his face or some kind of internal brain injury. What was clear? He was dying.

"Help . . . me . . ." The thin reedy voice was interrupted by weak coughing. "Escaped . . . prison . . . hide me . . . before guards . . . come."

"Nyx?" Posie called out. "What's happening?"

For a split second, Nyx couldn't think. No, that was a lie. She was thinking, just not about the car, the groceries, the kid who was dying or her hysterical sister.

"Where . . ." Nyx said urgently. "Where is the camp?"

Maybe after all these years... she could find out where Janelle had been taken.

This had to be Fate.

———◆———

"Hungry Like the Wolf" had apparently been released in December 1982 in the U.S. by the new wave, British sensation, Duran Duran. The video, working off an Indiana Jones theme, was put into heavy rotation on MTV, and that television airplay shot the song onto the Billboard charts and kept it there for months.

Whate'er all that meant.

As the Jackal whispered through the prison camp's subterranean tunnels, he was of the shadows, staying hidden as he tracked the song's tinny refrain while it echoed off the damp stone walls. He knew nothing personally of the "band" or the singer, but he had heard enough secondhand. Long had tales been related of a Simon Le Bon in a fedora and a pale linen suit hustling through crowded streets . . . then in the jungle, in the river . . . a beautiful woman pursuing him, or was it the other way around?

The fact that everything had been distilled unto

him by another, a representation of what was now, courtesy of time's passage, ancient news in and of itself, was a marked calendar of the century he'd spent down here in this hellhole. He knew nothing of MTV or this Le Bon fellow or, indeed, what a music video was.

But new inmates' recollections were the only updates one got from the outside world.

The world above, the freedom, the fresh air . . . they were like both the story of the video and the garbled sound of the song itself—dulled by time's passing and a lack of real-time refresh. And as with recollections of What Had Come Before or What Had Come Since, the rarity of the cassette player relic and that tape made both valuable beyond measure. Indeed, tangible ties to that of the up above were precious—and very fragile, given that they were subject to search and seizure as well as the entropy of repeated use.

The Jackal made a turn and entered one of the blocks of cells, the barred cages set at regular intervals in the rock, all the gated panels open. With the guards prowling around, monsters in the dark, there was no need to lock anything. No one dared to leave.

Death would be a blessing compared to what the Command would do to you.

The source of the ghostly song, now nearing the end of its run, was three cells down, and he stopped in the cell archway of the prisoner in question. "You get caught with that, they're going to—"

"Do what? Throw my ass in jail?"

The male who spoke was reclining on his pallet, his huge body in a relaxed sprawl, nothing but a cloth tied around his hips hiding his sex. Unblinking yellow eyes stared upward from the horizontal, and the sly smile showed long, sharp fangs.

"Just watching out for you." The Jackal nodded at the silver and black cassette player that was tucked into Lucan's side. "And your little machine."

"Everyone's at assembly, including the guards."

"You roll the dice too much, my friend."

"And you, Jackal, are too much of a rule abider."

That because I have something to lose, the Jackal thought.

As the song came to the end, Lucan hit the rewind button and there was a whirring sound. Then the soft music started up again.

"What are you going to do when that tape breaks?"

The wolven shrugged. "I have it now. That's all that matters."

The Jackal focused on the heavy collar of metal

that was locked around the male's thick throat. After everything the guy had been through, you couldn't blame him for only staying in the moment. Too far back or any second into the future? Experience had proven both to be a bad proposition.

"Better run along, Jackal." One of those yellow eyes winked. "Don't want to get in trouble."

"Just turn that thing down. I don't want to have to rescue you."

"Who's asking you to."

"Burdens of conscience."

"I wouldn't know about that."

"Lucky you." The Jackal turned away. "Life is a lot more complicated with them."

Leaving his comrade behind, he continued on, passing by more empty cells, and then taking the main tunnel unto the Hive. As he closed in on the mandatory assembly, the density of the air increased, the scents of the prisoners thick in the stillness—and the first of the screams sizzled into his ears well before he arrived, the high pitched sound pricking the hairs at the nape of his neck and tightening the powerful muscles of his shoulders.

As he emerged into the great open area, his eyes looked over the thousand heads, to the three blood-stained tree trunks that had been transplanted into the raised stone ledge far across the cave's vast expanse. The prisoner who was strapped to the center trunk writhed against the chains that held him in place, his bloodshot eyes wide with terror at the woven basket at his feet.

Something inside the basket was moving.

A pair of guards in clean black uniforms stood on either side of the accused, their faces set with the kind of deadly calm that a person should truly fear—because it meant they didn't value life in the slightest. Whether a prisoner lived or died was of no concern to them. They did their jobs, and went to their quarters each day secure in the knowledge that, whatever pain they caused, whatever destruction, whatever harm, had been done in the line of duty.

Therefore, no matter the depravity, their consciences were clear.

Something that stupid wolf needed to consider as he flouted the fucking rules like he did.

The ragged crowd was restless with adrenaline, bodies banging into each other as heads turned and talked and then refocused, eager for the show. These little "corrections" were given out by the Command on a regular basis, part bloodthirsty exhibition, part behavioral modification.

If you'd asked any of the prisoners, male or

female, they would have said they hated these regular public tortures, but they'd be lying—at least partially so. In the midst of the crushing boredom and soul-numbing hopelessness down here, the mandatory assemblies were breaks in the monotony.

A theatrical show that was everyone's favorite program.

Then again, it wasn't like there was much else on the schedule.

Unlike the rest of the prisoners, the Jackal shifted his eyes to one side of the ledge. He knew that the Control was there in person tonight—or mayhap it was today, he didn't know whether it was light or dark outside.

The presence of their leader was unusual and he wondered if anyone else noticed. Probably not. The Control was keeping itself hidden, but it liked these displays of its power.

As the lid on the basket was lifted by one of the guards, the Jackal looked down at his own feet and closed his eyes. The piercing scream that echoed around made the marrow of his bones ache. And then came the scent of fresh blood.

He had to get the fuck out of here. He was dying on the inside. He had no faith left. No love. No hope that anything would ever change.

It would take a miracle to free him.

But if his life had taught him anything, those acts of divinity never happened on earth. And rarely, if ever, up in heaven, either.

As the crowd began to chant, and all he could smell was that blood, he turned away from the spectacle and stumbled back into the tunnel.

Even in his despair, and in spite of the countless males and females packed into the cave, he could feel the eyes that followed his departure.

The Command watched him and him alone.

Always.

Chapter Two

As Rhage answered the most important question he was going to be presented for the evening, he was very aware that he was living his best frickin' life.

"Rocky Road. Definitely Rocky Road."

As he got out the two bowls and the two spoons that were Designated For Special Use, his daughter, Bitty, leaned into the old-school trunk freezer and snagged the half gallon in question. Then she narrowed her eyes on the thirty or so other choices for her own crucial decision.

"What are you feeling tonight?" he asked as he braced a hip on the counter and settled in.

You did not interfere in another's ice cream choice. No matter how long it took, no matter what the outcome, this was a sacred moment, a melding of mood and palate, whim and whimsy. Not to be rushed or influenced unduly by third-party outsiders, even fathers.

"What are we watching tonight?" his daughter asked.

For a moment, he got lost staring at her wavy brown hair and slender shoulders. She was wearing one of his black button-downs, and the thing was a full-length dress on her, the hem of the shirt reaching her ankles, the folds enveloping her like ceremonial robes. She'd rolled up the sleeves, and there was so much excess material she looked like she was wearing bat-winged baby waders for the pool. But she loved his shirts and he loved that she wanted to wear them.

In fact, he loved everything about his daughter, especially the way she looked up to him—and not just because he was three feet taller than her in his shitkickers. In her eyes, he was a superhero. A protector of the race. A fighter who took care of the innocent, the infirmed, the less capable.

The front line of defense between the species and any and all who would hurt them.

He felt stronger thanks to her. More powerful. Better prepared.

But not invincible. Oh, fuck no, on the invincibility. As with all things good, there was a balance, and when it came to Bitty, in spite of the purpose and strength she gave him, his daughter made him realize his mortality to painful degree.

He was more afraid of dying than ever before.

"Dad?"

Rhage shook himself back into focus. "Huh? Oh, the movie. I'm thinking *Zombieland Double Tap.*"

"Then mint chocolate chip." The decisiveness made Rhage smile. "And Ben and Jerry's, not the Breyers."

As Bitty palmed her choice and straightened, the glass door slid back into place with a bump, closing off the cold on a clap. "I'm not sure I need a bowl, though. This is just a pint."

Rhage glanced at what was in his left hand and was surprisingly disappointed. They always used the bowls and the spoons, which was why Fritz the butler kept the two pairs right here, in this far corner of the kitchen by the freezer. It was part of the ritual.

"Well, then I won't use one, either." He put the bowls aside, opened a drawer and got out two dish towels. "Let's wrap 'em up in this."

He tossed one to his daughter, gave her a spoon, and then after she passed him his half gallon, they were off, walking through the empty kitchen, outing via the pantry. As they emerged at the base of the foyer's grand staircase, he put a hand on Bits's shoulder.

"I'm glad I'm off tonight."

"Me, too, Dad. How's your foot? Are you okay?"

"Oh, yeah. No worries." He kept the pain and the limp to himself. "Bone's going to heal just fine. Manny took care of it."

"He's a good person."

"He is."

Together, they went up the red carpeted steps. In spite of the Your Majesty decor, with all that gold leafing and the crystal, the marble columns and the painted ceiling high above, this was home. This was where the Black Dagger Brotherhood lived with their families and took care of Wrath, Beth, and L.W. This was where the best lives for all of them transpired, here under this heavy roof, here behind these stout stone walls, here . . . protected by the *mhis* that Vishous threw.

A fortress.

A fucking vault, which was where precious things belonged, safe from theft or destruction.

The movie theater was on the second floor, out past the Hall of Statues, through the other side at the head of the staff wing. Given that it was after twelve on a work night, no one was around. Those fighters who were on rotation were out in the field. The injured who needed rehab were down in the training center. And the staff were on break to eat after having cooked, served, and cleaned up First Meal. Meanwhile, Mary was in session with Zsadist down in the basement. Wrath and Beth were play-ing with L.W. up on the third floor. And the other *shellans* and kiddos were in the bouncy castle out by the pool on the back terrace.

So it was nice and quiet. Cool, too, in all the air-conditioning.

Plus, yeah, the movie theater was a professional gig for real: Stadium seating with padded leather ass-palaces. A candy counter and popcorn machine maintained, as everything was, by Fritz. A huge screen framed by red velvet drapes that had just been updated. Dolby surround sound and then some, with the kind of woofers that made you feel the T. rex's footfalls in *Jurassic Park* all the way through your torso.

Rhage and Bitty took the two seats right in the middle, halfway up the rows. It was where they'd sat the night before, so the remotes to the computer system were in the drink cup holder between them.

Work of a moment to rent the movie on Amazon and get things rolling.

As they popped their ice cream lids and settled in to put their spoons to work, Rhage exhaled long and slow.

Perfect. This was just—

"Cheers, Dad."

He looked over. Bitty was holding out her spoon, and Rhage clinked his against it. "Cheers, daughter."

In the dark, as the adventure of the movie began, Rhage smiled so wide that he forgot about the ice cream. Everything was right in the world. All circles completed. Nothing gray in any area of his life.

He had his daughter.

He had his beloved *shellan*.

He had his brothers and his buddies.

Yes, there was stress and the threat to the species continued and the fucking humans were always up to shit. But he felt like his life was similar to this fortress of a house.

Solid against the storms and assaults of Fate.

Capable of withstanding anything that was thrown at it.

It was the first and only time he had ever felt like this, and it made him believe, deep in his bones, that no matter what, nothing was going to change.

And what a wonderful thing that was.

Digging into his Rocky Road, he had no idea what was coming his way. If he had, he would have chosen a much different ice cream.

Like motherfucking vanilla.

1991